8.

'When it's time,
it's time."

By
Luing Andrews
&
Jack East

Copyright © 2020 Luing Andrews
All rights reserved.

DEDICATION

This book is dedicated to my wife and family.

CONTENTS

Acknowledgments

Chapter One

Chapter Two

Chapter Three

Chapter Four

Chapter Five

Chapter Six

Chapter Seven

Chapter Eight

Chapter Nine

Chapter Ten

Chapter Eleven

Chapter Twelve

Chapter Thirteen

Chapter Fourteen

Chapter Fifteen

ACKNOWLEDGMENTS

Thanks to Jack East.

"Copyright © 2020 Luing Andrews

All rights reserved. No part of this publication may be reproduced, distributed, or transmitted in any form or by any means, including photocopying, recording, or other electronic or mechanical methods, without the prior written permission of the publisher, except in the case of brief quotations embodied in critical reviews and certain other noncommercial uses permitted by copyright law. For permission requests, go to the address below."

https://www.facebook.com/8ishNovel

This book is a work of fiction and should be read with that in mind. Characters, places, real people and historical events have been used fictitiously. Other names, characters, places, and incidents are the products of the authors imagination and any resemblance to persons living or dead or places is purely coincidental.

ONE

Sean had known this estate for too many years. Although he had friends around him, they never made it feel like it was his home.

Sixties housing estates, like this one, grew two things.

Crime and criminals.

The outside world didn't exist for most of its inhabitants. To many of them, their lives were defined by the small puddle they lived in.

Over the years, a few legendary people had escaped their tiny existence but most of its inhabitants just tried to survive.

For Sean, it felt like he was caged in with the prey, not the predators.

As people walked past his house, he dragged on his cigarette and stared at their tiny lives unfolding in front of him. To him, they all looked like insects under a microscope.

He was an apex predator. Top of the food chain. King of the world.

How had he ended up living this shitty existence when he knew how royalty could live.

He flicked his butt into the street and turned to go back indoors.

"Fucking rats in a cage" he said and closed the door behind him.

TWO

As he climbed the stairs, he could see through the doorway into the kitchen. On the floor next to the table was a blood stain that looked like a map of Ireland. "Ironic," he thought, considering his family heritage. The O'Sheas had left their homeland a few generations ago but their veins still pumped with five-hundred years of fighting blood.

The claret on the tiles wasn't his, although, he was the one that spilt it. Sean remembered looking through the window the previous evening and seeing his wife, laying on the table, legs spread and moaning under the weight of Petes shabby body. Scattered around her were small bags of coke which Sean guessed were left overs from Pete's evening dealing drugs to the local trash.

Jean had been struggling to focus on the sex. "Come on Pete, do me" she said, but that wasn't what she cared about. Within reach were a couple of packets of white powder with the words "Supply & Demand" printed on the plastic. Pete's jog pants were half way down his thighs and the same words were tattooed on his bare arse cheeks. Well, two of them were, Sean had no idea where the "&" sign was but it wasn't visible. Jean pushed her body back at Pete just enough to be able to reach the packets. She held them tight, hoping he hadn't seen. Pete misread her intentions thinking she was desperate for him. "Dirty slag," he thought, "she's gagging for it. Better give her what she wants." And he started banging harder, getting closer to the short strokes. In any other life, he would never get near a woman as good looking as this but, because he controlled the little white powder, he could make her do anything he wanted. He smiled, not from pleasure, but because he enjoyed dragging her into his world.

Behind him the door exploded and Pete's smile disappeared in a second. Sean was slightly above average height but he had spent his life building functional muscle. It wasn't there to look good, it was there to protect him if needed, to damage others if pushed and to kill if required. He didn't know which one it would be used for right now, he never did. Whatever it turned out to be was up to the other person. Go down easy and you can walk away, go down hard and you probably wouldn't get up again.

Pete looked terrified and struggled back trying to pull up his pants. Before he got them up Sean hit him with a sucker punch to the underside of his jaw. It lifted him a foot into the air and the bone shattered immediately. Pete hit the cupboard and then the floor. Jean tried to climb off of the table and get her skirt down from around her waist. "It wasn't me, he offered me some coke if I let him," she screamed.

Sean looked down at her and felt sick seeing what she had become. He had always wanted the best for her, even though he knew she was badly damaged inside. Over the years he had saved her from an abusive ex, her parents and more recently, the local dealers. Now he realised he couldn't save her from herself. His anger turned to pity.

Behind him, Pete tried to struggle to his feet. Sean looked over his shoulder. His voice was quiet but carried menace in every syllable. "If you get up, you are going down," he said.

Pete couldn't reply, his jaw was trying to cope with moving four pieces of bone instead of one. The left side hung at an ugly angle. Out of his jacket pocket he pulled a flick knife. The blade sprung into view as he staggered to his feet.

Sean's muscles tensed. Time to go to work.

As Pete slashed the blade in front of him, he had lost the fight before it even started. Stiletto blades are good for stabbing, not cutting. Sean grabbed Pete's wrist, turned the knife, and used it for what it was built. He drove it in just below the collar bone. Before a scream hit the air, he dropped a head-butt into Pete's face and the room fell silent. A small pool of blood spread across the floor next to the dealers unconscious body.

He turned to Jean and stared at her for a second. "I'm done. Clean this shit up before the boys wake up. You can have the house and the money, but if anything happens to my kids before I come and get them, your body will never be found."

Sean shook off the memory of the previous evening. He continued up the stairs, grabbed a bag and stuffed a few pieces in. Before he walked back down he lifted a tile in the bathroom just above the sink. Hidden above the pipes was a silver revolver and a box of .44 shells. He put them in the holdall and started to go down stairs.

"That's right, just leave. You always wanted to," shouted Jean from the lounge. "You are pathetic!"

"Remember what I said. I don't care what you do with your life, but if you mess up the boys with your shit before I come back, you and your dealer are dead."

Jean ran to the door and pinned herself to it stopping Sean leaving. "Please," she was in tears "Don't leave."

"You left years ago Jean. I'm just doing the same thing." He pulled her away, stepped through the door and slid into the night.

THREE

"Bollocks!" Sean had been driving for an hour through weather as bleak as his mood. He couldn't remember the last thirty miles, partly because of his thoughts but mostly because of the rain. It had been hammering against the windscreen so hard he could have imagined he was in a car wash. Now a yellow warning light on the Jeep's dash suddenly dragged him back into the real world. It was shaped like a petrol pump and had triggered a ding from a hidden speaker in the dashboard.

"Bloody hell." Sean looked at the motorway ahead and wondered how many miles he had left in the tank. 10 minutes later, a sign on the verge promised petrol in another 3 miles. He pulled onto the forecourt and sat staring at the rain with the engine running for a few minutes. In front of him, a compact family hatchback full of kids was filling up with petrol. Small faces filled the rear window and hands began waving towards him. He waved back and smiled but his mood didn't improve. The last time he had seen his sons he was getting into his car to leave. They had heard Jean screaming at their dad, begging him to stay. As he had thrown his bag in the backseat they waved to him. He had waved back, just like he was waving now. His mood darkened even more. Sean needed to get them back and soon. To do that he needed cash and not just the travelling money he had with him.

As the car loaded with kids pulled out, he fished in his pocket for his wallet. Sean pulled out a wad of notes and something fluttered free. A small card had fallen into his lap.

On the front and in small red letters it said "8ish"

while on the back it had the words "Club & Bar". Below that, in fainter lettering, was a telephone number, an address in Soho and a picture of a Champagne glass. He left it sitting on the dashboard while he filled up and paid. As he climbed back behind the wheel he saw it propped up above the steering wheel like a little tombstone laid on its back. Sean picked it up and stared down at it, his fingers tracing around the edge of the figure 8. He noticed he was still wearing his wedding ring. His anger swelled enough for him pull it off, drop the window for a second and launched it towards a drain. Sean looked back at the card.

"Fuck it, no choice." If he pushed hard he could be in Soho around 8ish. The irony wasn't lost on him but his grim expression was still set in stone. Going home never made him as happy as it should.

He started the engine, accelerated into the traffic and took the turn towards London.

Theresa O'Shea hated mornings. Especially mornings when she had to get up early. Today was different. Today she had nothing planned except a lay in until noon. Theresa loved lay-ins. She turned onto her side, pulled the duvet over her head and settled in to enjoy her morning just as the doorbell rang. "For fuck sake." She decided she wasn't home and pulled the sheets tighter. Then the bell started ringing continuously. After a minute she gave up and slid out of bed and into a dressing gown.

As she walked down the stairs, she could see a massive shadow the other side of the glass door. Either someone had delivered a wardrobe or Arnold Schwarzenegger had dropped by for a coffee.

Teresa opened the lock and swung the door open. Facing away from her was a muscular shape in a leather jacket and jeans.

"Can I help you?" she said.

"I hope so," said Sean turning to face his sister.

In an instant she was awake and wrapping her arms around her brother. Theresa was shrieking at the top of her voice. "Oh my god, you're back!"

Eventually she dropped out of his arms and stepped back pressing her finger to her lips in a conspiratorial way. "Shush," she said and grabbed his hand, leading him into the house. At the entrance to the kitchen Theresa pushed Sean ahead of her.

Their mum stood at the sink wiping dishes. "Was it the post love?"

"Yes, am I what you were expecting?" said Sean.

"Sean?" said his mum "God where have you been?" Audrey looked down and saw his finger with a pale white band where a ring should be. She looked up. "Ah, fuck. What has she done now?"

"I've left her mum. I need a place to stay until I can sort things out."

"You look like crap son."

"That's what sleeping in a car will do to you. I got stuck in traffic and I didn't want to go to the club that late or wake you up so I decided to kip in the motor."

"You should have come home. It didn't matter what time it was," said Audrey "that slut was never your type."

"Don't start mum."

"I'll talk about her whatever way I want," she said but instantly dropped her eyes to the floor. In the hallway it looked like the lights had started to go out. A large shape blotted out the corridor and moved into the kitchen. Audrey stepped back, trying make herself small and inconspicuous.

"Are you being a disrespectful shit-head?"

Sean turned and saw a man as big as him step out of the shadows. "I wasn't dad, and if you ever call me a shit-head again it will be the last words you say. I'm not the boy you used to kick around."

"So you are a big man now?"

"I was a big man before I left but I didn't fuck with you out of respect. Those days are gone. You need to hold your peace or I will feed it to you in spades. I don't have the patience, the time or the gene pool to cut you any slack Ray."

"I'm not Ray, I'm your fucking dad."

"Blood doesn't make you my dad," said Sean as he met his father halfway. They stood with their faces inches apart. Sean imagined dropping a head butt between Rays eyes, but as the thought crossed his mind Audrey shouted "Alright. Alright, for fuck sake. Enough of this. Not even fifteen minutes with the O'Shea men under the same roof without a brawl."

Sean stared down the old man and used his bulk to push past him. "I need a bath ma," he said.

"Yes darling, go up now. You know where everything is. I'll get some breakfast on for you. Bacon and eggs alright?" Sean nodded and walked up the stairs past his dad. As he got to his sister he smiled as if to say everything was ok. But it wasn't. Everything was wrong and Sean needed to sort it in quick order if he was ever going to get his sons back again.

Sean held the handle of his old room, turned it clockwise and pushed. Thirty years disappeared in a second. As he stepped inside the half-lit room, it wasn't the small changes which stood out but how much was still the same. The colour of paint had changed but the Lonsdale gloves and his boxing trophies still lay on the shelf. They were all from his early teens. There were no trophies for the real matches he had fought years later when the gloves were off.

To his right, a long glass fronted wardrobe reflected his old room in a distorted parody of its old self. He dropped his bag on the bed, pulled a small chair towards the mirrored doors and stood on its seat. As he reached over the top his hand easily slipped down the back. For an instant, his fingers grasped at fresh air but then they found it. Sean stepped down, walked towards the window and into the light. As he lifted the rectangle of card and blew, a picture of a topless page 3 girl appeared from under the dust. He turned it over and did the same on the back. In faded blue ink an equation appeared. "26+6=1". He blew again and some words were slowly uncovered. "If you don't stand for something you will fall for anything." Below that and surrounding the letters IRA, it finished "Our time will come."

"It came and went," he said out loud. The dream of uniting the Republics 26 counties with Northern Irelands 6 to make 1 unified country was long gone. In hindsight, he often wondered if it had ever been an honest ambition or if it was driven by more basic needs. Since the war had ended, life had prospered in the country on both sides of the border but during the troubles his family had gained notoriety, status and money.

In the bottom right hand corner was an enamel pin. It was green with four leaves and surrounded by silver edging.

He ran his fingers over the metal. This cheap piece of tin had cost him. It even cost the lives of some of his friends. Sean ripped the pin out of the card, threw the picture into the bin, and headed for the shower.

Twenty minutes later he started back down the stairs, cleaner, lighter in the shoulders and nearly carrying a smile.

As he got to the bottom Ray ran past him clutching a jacket and a set of car keys. "See you later love," he shouted behind him.

He heard his mum in the kitchen "What, where are you going? Aren't you going to help me today?" Before her words ended the door slammed shut and Ray was gone.

"Bloody great," she said as Sean walked through the door and sat down at the table and started eating. Audrey sat down opposite him "Off with that bloody mob, up to no good."

"Same one mum?"

"Yes same one. Complete bunch of useless bastards they always were."

"So how have you been ma?"

"I'm ok Sean. What else should I be?"

"Look, I have to pop out to sort a few things if that's ok? Do you need me to get you anything while I'm out?"

"No thanks Sean. Its all good."

"Thanks for breakfast, it was perfect." He stood up from the table, pulled on his leather jacket and walked towards the door.

"Sean," said Audrey. Her son stopped for a second and turned "It's great to have you home."

For the first time in two days Sean smiled completely. He winked at his mum turned back around and headed to the door. Before he could get to it, his sister raced down the stairs and smothered him with kisses.

"I'm so happy you're back." She stepped away and punched him hard in the chest just as Audrey caught up with them.

"What the hell is that for?" He said.

"For staying away so long."

Audrey punched him as well.

"Really? I have come home to have the women of the house beat me up?"

"Then don't be such a stranger," said Audrey.

The loud bang on the door ended the moment as quickly as it had started.

Audrey walked to the door and started turning the catch. "It will be your da. He's always forgetting stuff nowadays."

The door opened and without asking a younger version of Ray stepped into the house. Like a steam train rolling into a siding, he left a trail of smoke behind him.

"Auntie Audrey!" he said as he manoeuvred the cigar around his mouth. The fake enthusiasm disappeared as he asked "Where is he?"

"Danny? Who are you talking…"

Sean stepped out from behind the door. "It's ok ma. Ray has a big mouth as well as an empty head."

"And a mobile phone," said Danny. The fake enthusiasm was back. "He was so happy to see you he gave me a bell to spread the good news. Welcome back lad." He leant forward and grabbed Seans hand. The two men stared at each other. Sean had neither the inclination or need to blow smoke up Danny's arse after all these years and his expression told his cousin exactly that. After ten seconds with their hands locked together, Dans shit eating grin slowly slipped away.

In an effort to avoid losing face he turned and pointed down the short path to a large black Mercedes parked at the curb. "Come say hello to an old friend." Without waiting Danny pulled Sean towards the car and the driver's window dropped down. Behind it was a chirpy young man who instantly waved. "Sean!"

"Mickey!" Sean walked over and grabbed him with real warmth. "How the hell are you?"

Before he could answer Danny joined them and opened the back door. "Come on Sean, lets go for a drive and we can catch up on old times while we travel."

"Where we going?"

"The club Sean, the club of course. You have people that want to see you again." The over-done enthusiasm was back but it was a thin veneer over the underlying menace it covered.

Sean waved goodbye to Theresa and his mum, climbed into the limo and disappeared behind the smoked window as the car instantly pulled away.

FOUR

The seats were made of leather that told your arse it was sitting on something high grade not man made. Around the doors mood lighting picked up each piece of chrome and reflected a violet glow onto every panel. Up front, Mickey occasionally glanced in the mirror and smiled. Beside Sean, Dan had lost all of the friendly charm he had spent so much work portraying.

"Why are you back?"

"Personal reasons. Why do you want to know."

"We just want to know your intentions."

"Who is we? Is it you and Mickey or does someone else want to know?"

"Dad wants to know." Dan tried to seem indifferent that his father was showing an interest in his cousins return.

"Then I will tell Bill when I see him. I guess that's where we are going."

"Sure is," said Mickey. "He's at the club waiting."

"Shut up Mickey. I'm having the discussion with Sean. After all, we have known each other for a long time."

"I'll talk to Bill first," said Sean. "I need to clear the air."

"A lot has changed since you left Sean. I run most of the business now. Bill trusts *me* now."

"So why has he sent for me rather than have you talk to me instead?"

"I am talking to you."

"No, you are my Uber. He sent you to bring me to him. Nothing more."

Dan looked out of the window and stared into the distance. "As I said, a lot has changed. Best you remember that Sean. Your ship sailed a long time ago. It sailed and then sank without a fucking trace."

The rest of the journey was spent in silence. Even Mickey decided not to try and break the tension. It wasn't worth the potential damage. Best to let Sean talk to Bill before he got in the middle of this pissing contest.

At the club, Mickey pulled into a parking place at the side of the building.

The three of them climbed out and walked through the giant red doors. Over the top, it had a massive neon sign that said "8ish" and then underneath, in smaller letters, it continued "Till Late". The glow made everyone's face look like it was covered in blood.

Inside, the place was dark with occasional pools of light over tables and behind the bar. Swimming in the pools were sharks and fish. Some were playing poker and others just discussing business. Sean remembered the serious card players always liked to think of themselves as apex predators. The sharks. Anyone else at the table was a fish. They were people who had more money than sense or ones that thought they could gamble their way into the big-time. Either way, they paid for the comfortable lifestyle the sharks enjoyed. Occasionally a fish got lucky but then there were other ways to make certain the money never made it out of the club.

As Dan, Mickey and Sean walked through to the back, the conversations at the tables died as they passed. As soon as the O`Sheas were out of ear shot new conversations started, mostly concerning Sean's return.

Towards the back, a mixture of heavies and bar staff watched the procession pass. At the office door

Dan knocked and walked in. Mickey stepped to one side and let Sean walk ahead on his own.

Behind a desk the size of a small aircraft carrier was a man in his early 70's. He wore a three piece suit that was wrapped around old, thick, sinewy muscles. The man looked up at Sean and then across to Dan who was about to sit in a large leather chair.

"Wait outside."

"What?" Dan looked like he had been told to fix his lipstick.

"I said wait outside, or was I being too subtle. How about this, fuck off Dan, I want to talk to Sean alone."

Danny started to open his mouth and then decided now wasn't the time. He walked towards the door and had to pass his cousin on the way. "Do me a favour," said Sean. "Get me a cup of water while you are waiting big man. Oh, and while you are there you might as well heat it up, pop in a tea bag and a drop of milk."

Dan stepped into Sean's face wearing a look as black as coal. "I'm not your fucking tea boy."

"Danny!" Bill's voice left no room for negotiation.

He stepped around Sean's immobile body and closed the door. As he shut it, Mickey was leant against the wall. "Not staying bruv?"

"Mickey, I know you like your cousin but you are still my little brother and that only gives you so many get out of jail free cards, so stop sucking his cock the minute after he gets back. Pick the right side of the road or get run over." Dan pushed passed him and headed for the bar.

"Tosser," said Mickey making certain his older brother couldn't hear.

Back inside the room, Bill stepped out from behind

the desk sliding something heavy into the back of his waistband. He walked towards Sean and stopped less than a foot from his nose. They stared at each other for what seemed like an eternity but, in reality, probably only lasted ten seconds.

"Come back cap in hand have you boy?" said Bill.

Sean grabbed his uncle's fist. It felt more like a warm side of beef than a person's hand. "I did bring one thing old man." Sean jammed something inside and closed Bill's fingers over it.

As he looked down and opened his hand he saw the metal shamrock sitting in his palm. Bill looked up and burst out laughing. He kept laughing until a coughing fit overwhelmed him. "I never thought I would see this again."

"I never thought I would have to give it back," said Sean.

"So you want to cash in a favour? Ok what do you want?" said Bill.

"Work. Money. A future."

"You had all of that before and walked away from it."

"For my kids."

"So why are you back now?"

"For my kids."

"It's funny how men sacrifice their principles for their blood isn't it? Ok. You have a job. But I don't want to hear any arguments about what it is. I tell you what to do and you say yes. No being fussy. Understand?"

"Sure."

"Be here at nine in the morning and I will give you instructions. Mickey, Dan!" shouted Bill.

The door opened and both of his sons walked in.

"Good news, Sean is back in the business."

Mickey's face lit up and Danny's turned black.

"Take him out and introduce him to the staff Mickey. Sean, take this with you." Bill slid a 9mm automatic from behind his back and pushed it into his nephews hand. He looked down at it, felt the weight and slipped it into his jacket pocket.

"Sean?"

"Yes Bill."

"You didn't need to call in a favour, you are blood boy. You will always have a home here." The two smiled and then Mickey walked him back to the bar.

Dan watched Sean walk out of the room and turned to his dad. "Already forgotten he fucked off without a word? Piece of shit! Everyones already all over him. It's pathetic."

"I don't know whats between you two but I want it to stop. He's our family and that's the end of it."

"He turned his back on us."

"And now he's back and I'm glad so pipe down. Lets put him to work and see if he still has what it takes to be an O`Shea."

Dan walked out into the bar and watched Sean and Mickey talking to some of the bouncers. They were laughing like they were old friends. "There is only one O`Shea family and you are not it," said Danny. He pulled a phone out of his pocket and redialled the last number. "He's been welcomed back. I need you to keep an eye on him. He needs to be managed or things could go wrong." Dan ended the call and watched Mickey walk his cousin to the car. He rubbed the handgrip of the revolver under his jacket. It felt solid and serious. The metal handle was something to be relied upon. Something comforting. Something which gave him respect. Well until today. Sean had taken some of that respect and stamped on it. His dad had welcomed the fucker back. His brother was having a bromance and now Sean was creeping back into *the business*. The business he had run for two years while his cousin was off playing happy families. Something had to be done and soon, before Bill got any ideas about who was in charge.

The next morning, Sean was back in Bill's office. He sat at the giant desk, which only had three things on it's mahogany top. A set of car keys with an 8ish logo on the key fob was sat next to a sheet of paper with some writing on it and on top of a box of 124 grain Winchester PDX1 DEFENDER bullets.

"Why the cannon shells?"

"Better safe than sorry. These things will carve a hole into someone the size of the Channel Tunnel. No need to worry. No one gets up after a Defender hits them."

"Are you having problems?"

"No more than normal, but I want you to carry when you are on O`Shea business."

"Ok. What's on the paper?"

"Your jobs for the day. Think of it as an audition."

"I thought I was family."

"Yes you are but even family has to work and show they can be trusted."

Sean picked up the items on the desk and headed towards the rear exit.

"Did I ever tell you the best piece of advice my mum gave me Sean"'

"No Bill. What did she say."

"When I left home she said I should always

remember one rule in life."

"What was that?"

"She said *don't be stupid*. Good advice Sean." The tone in Bill's voice was unmistakable. "No fuckups. Ok?"

Sean nodded, opened the door and stepped into the bright morning light."

At the end of the alley, a woman was leaning against the wall. Her clothes were dirty, her hair unwashed for weeks and a layer of dirt covered her hands. The skin on her face was thin and emaciated due to a decade of heroin use. She lifted her head as the big guy exited the rear of the club and climbed into the Range Rover. As he pulled away the prostitute lifted a brand new mobile phone to her ear.

"He's left," she said. "Heading north east."

As Sean's 4x4 turned right at the end of the road, a beat up old ford pulled away from the curb and melted into the traffic behind him.

The Range Rover sat idling against the curb, 15 feet away from the newsagent's whose address was written on the paper. Next to the shop was an estate agent's window full of central London loft apartments. Sean flipped down the sun-visor. On the reverse side it had a sticker which announced DOCTOR ON CALL in inappropriately large letters.

He stepped out and walked into the lettings agency.

"How can I help you?" said a young man in a dark grey suit and lavender tie who looked like he was auditioning for a business reality show.

"I need two Dona Kebabs and three portions of chips," said Sean.

Behind the walking Dragons Den interviewee, the rest of the room erupted in laughter.

"But…"

"But what? Why are you asking a man in a lettings agency what he wants? You don't see that it is a fucking stupid question?"

"No, er, what I meant was…"

"What you meant was, I am going to waste your time building a rapport rather than getting to the point. Why do you want to build a rapport? Because you want to rent me some overpriced piece of crap. Now we know where we are perhaps we can save each other some time. I want a central London gaff with three bedrooms."

Lavender tie was immediately out of his depth. "We have several very attractive bijou properties we can show you," he stammered.

Sean looked around the room and found an old face he remembered. "Hello Chris, you know me?"

"Yes Sean, I remember."

"Good, then get this twat away from me."

Chris was in his early fifties and had seen the East End change beyond belief. When he was a kid, it was the tail end of the Krays and Richardsons. Ganglands elite. Now it was full of Yuppies and bankers serviced by people in lavender ties like Hugo.

"Fuck off Hugo," said Chris. "Before you get yourself into real trouble."

"Chris," said Hugo "we have a policy that says we don't have to put up with abusive customers."

"Hugo, we also have an unwritten policy that we don't piss off people who will burn our houses down in the middle of the night while we are in them or any people that will magically make our kneecaps disappear. Now fuck off before I let our new customer explain it to you in vivid detail, you useless tosser."

"Do you have something for me? Somewhere near a good school?"

"We do but they are really expensive. It's changed around here Sean."

"What do you call expensive?"

"Even if I get you a great deal you won't get much change out of two grand a month for a safe area with a good school and away from local gangs."

"Fuck me!"

"Do you want me to keep an eye out?"

"Thanks Chris. Please let me know. I appreciate it." Sean handed him a small piece of paper with a phone number on it. "If I can do you a favour in return, you let me know."

"No problems. Happy to help."

"One last thing. I want the local scum to know I'm back. Tell a few stories, spread the word. You know. I need people to realise their world has changed and I'm their worst nightmare."

"Should I exaggerate to put the fear of God in them?"

"Do you need to?"

Chris remembered back two decades. He had heard the stories about Sean. How he was when he drank and why he stopped. He could still visualise Sean losing his shit in the local and the bloody aftermath he had left. The men never seen again. The ones walking with sticks. A couple who would never talk again.

"No Sean, no need to exaggerate."

"Appreciated Chris."

Sean got up and shook the old mans hand.

"By the way Sean. What's the deal with the back up car?"

"What?"

"The shit box Ford outside with the two guys watching us. Are we in trouble?"

Sean looked over Chris's shoulder and into the glossy picture behind him. In the dark parts he could see the reflection of a car and the driver looking directly at him.

"No, no trouble. I'll deal with it."

He let go of the estate agents hand and walked to the door. After opening it he turned left and headed towards the door of the newsagents. As he walked in he saw a mid twenties, mixed race guy standing behind the counter. He wore a tight T-Shirt, deliberately designed to show off a decade of hard work in the gym.

"How can I help you?"

Sean thought about Hugo next door and decided it must be a standard piece of customer service training.

"I'm here to pick up the payment."

The big guy stood up and flexed his muscles in an obvious attempt to intimidate. "I told the last guy. Times are hard. We'll pay when we have more cash in the till. So until then, you will just have to go fuck yourself. I can't pay if I don't have it."

Sean looked over his shoulder and saw the Ford had rolled back twenty feet so the occupants could see into the shop. He turned back to the weight lifter. "Do you know me?"

"No, I haven't seen you before."

"So you don't know what you are dealing with."

"And neither do you. I have had new business

associates in and they tell me they will take care of you if I pay them half what Bill asks. They say the O`Sheas are ancient history so why don't you do one." As if to prove he was in the driving seat, he stepped around the counter and into the Irishman's face.

Sean knew there were eyes on him from the street and it was time to make an example. Unfortunately for this guy he had just volunteered. In a flash, Sean dropped a head-butt between the big man's eyes. His nose exploded and the bridge shattered into a dozen pieces. Blood filled his throat and tears streamed down his cheeks. In an instant he couldn't see or breath.

Stepping back so that the blood spray wouldn't hit his jacket, Sean slammed a fist into the guys ribs breaking the two lowest ones. As the man started to fall he followed him down with an elbow drop onto the man's collar bone. The noise of it breaking filled the room. Now on his knees in front of the Irishman, the shop keeper desperately swung a left fist into mid air. Sean caught it and twisted it back breaking the wrist just above the joint.

In the Ford, the man's scream could be clearly heard.

As the man lay on the floor, he held his arm and began begging for the beating to end.

"My name is Sean O'Shea. I'm back and I'm not to be fucked with. Danny might be a soft touch but from now on you deal with me. Understand?"

"Yes, fuck yes. Please…"

"Tell everyone I did this to you. If they want to be able to wipe their own arse without asking a nurse to help them, they had better fucking heed the warning. Now, WHERE IS THE FUCKING MONEY?"

The man desperately pointed to the counter.

Under there in the coffee tin.

Sean leant over, pulled out there hundred pounds and dropped the rest on the floor. As he left he said "See you in two weeks. Be ready and don't be a twat. By the way, you might want to tell the other crew who are trying to muscle in they had better have big fucking balls."

He walked into the street, climbed into the car and drove away.

Across the road a car door opened. The passenger stepped around the Ford and walked towards the newsagents. He looked through the open door and inspected the big man lying in a pool of his own blood. He scanned the room and noted the level of devastation. Then he walked back to the car. Climbing in he settled in his seat and looked over at the driver. "The stories aren't bullshit. He's a fucking animal."

"So what do we do?"

"We are supposed to verify that he is the real deal. Job done. Let's piss off back to the club and report to Dan."

"What about Bill?"

"We'll tell him after. Dan wants us to know he is in charge."

"Dan's a mentalist. He isn't a patch on his dad."

"That's right and because he is standing on a thin ledge he will be a hundred times more dangerous. He's a wounded animal backed into a corner. Don't fuck with him."

"What about Mickey?"

"He's a nice kid but he's not a stone cold killer."

"So what do we do?"

"Our jobs. We report to Bill, but it doesn't cause a

big problem if we keep Dan in the loop first. Beyond that, we make certain we don't piss off Sean unless we want to end up like the guy across the street, or worse than that, never to be seen again."

"Is Sean that bad?"

His partner looked across at him. "Let me tell you this. I'm happy to take a couple of mates with me to deal with any nasty bastard. If I was going to confront Sean, I would take a dozen men and I would want all of them to be carrying."

"Bullshit!"

"Bullshit it is not my friend, now go over to the shop and pick up the money laying on the floor."

The driver's door opened and the young man walked across the street. After a minute he came back empty handed. He leaned into the window and shrugged. "Why did he leave the cash?"

"Why didn't you pick it up?"

"Because it was left there for a reason and I didn't want to piss off Sean."

"Great, you are learning. Now get in the fucking car and let's go back to the club.

As Sean manoeuvred the black Range Rover around the streets stopping at each address on Bills piece of paper, every job became easier. His violent approach to announcing his return had set light to a wildfire on the local information network. Just as he had planned. Better to set an example with one person than to have a hundred stupid confrontations. Now he had one last job to do before he could head back to the club. He looked at the address and a hand scribbled note next to it that said "squatter". Sean's assumption was that some druggies had decided to dig their heels in to avoid having to find another place to deal from.

As he pulled up outside he looked at the address and realised he was at a basement flat. "Druggy rats hiding underground." He did not knock but instead kicked the door wide and made a point of slamming it hard to signal bad shit was in town and heading towards the occupants of the flat.

He headed down some steps to a basement door and banged so hard the hinges rattled. "Open the door or I will kick it in by the count of three." As he said two the lock clicked free and it swung two inches away from the frame.

Sean pushed the door with his foot to make certain there wasn't a baseball bat waiting in the shadows. "Step into the light and hand over the cash you fucking vermin, then you need to pack up and go."

A small woman slid from behind the door. In the distance two small children peered around the corner.

For an instant, Sean saw his boys looking at him from the living room, then he shrugged it off and got back to the job.

"You need to leave."

"But I have some money coming soon. Their useless fucking dad promised me he would send some this week."

"Bill couldn't give a fuck. This place needs to be empty today."

"Please, give me another week. I can stay with my friend in a few days. She will help me but I need to have a place for us until the weekend."

The two kids had crept up behind their mum and were hiding behind her.

"Please…"

"For fucks sake. Where are the keys?"

She handed them over and Sean unwound the largest one hanging from the metal ring.

"Take this and get a new one cut. See the brick in the corner of the drive? Put the original under there tonight and then leave. When it gets dark, come back and you can stay until Sunday. After that I will do my job properly. Don't think otherwise."

The young woman looked at the children. "Go and watch TV for a minute." She pushed them away and they shuffled into the back room. "Can I thank you? They will stay downstairs. We could go up and.. ...you know. I could repay you."

Sean looked at the kids sitting watching TV. They were close to his boys age. Right now they might be watching TV while their mum was *thanking* Pete upstairs.

"No need. Keep them safe and if anyone tries to hurt them find me." His face was dark and, as much as he was trying to help her, the young mother was terrified by what was hidden behind his eyes.

When he left, she unclenched her fingers and realised her palms were wet with sweat. The young woman watched as the door closed behind him.

She clasped the rosary around her neck and pressed it to her chest. "Thank you for sending a good man but God help anyone in his way." Her shoulders dropped and her grip relaxed. As much as she was happy to have met him, she was relieved to be out from under the gaze of those dark blue eyes.

"Come on you two. We need to pack. At the weekend we are leaving."

"Was he helping us mum? He seemed nice."

"Yes, he was helping us. I think he liked you too."

She picked up the key, slid it into her pocket and let

herself into the street as she went to get a new one cut. As she passed a big black 4x4 as she failed to notice Sean was at the wheel and talking on the phone. "I'll meet you at the Airport, say six… …no, they can eat with me of course. Oh, and cheers for this, I owe you one. Later."

Five miles away, Dan was leaning on the bar talking to a young woman in her early twenties. She was wearing a top that was so low that it nearly showed her bellybutton. "Best dress code I ever came up with," he thought. As she leant forward to put a drink in front of him he made no effort to hide the fact he was staring straight at her breasts. The two men from the Ford walked through the club and straight over to where he was sitting. "We followed him Dan. Thought you would want to know what happened before we go and tell Bill."

Dan never took his eyes of her chest as he said, "So, what did he do when he got to the newsagents. That guy is useful, he boxed for years as a semi pro?"

"He won't be boxing anymore unless he can do it one-handed. Your cousin is a meat grinder on legs and that bloke got turned into sausages."

Dan broke away from the girls thrupennies and stared at the men. "What did he do?"

"Beat him bad. Broke an arm I think and left him in a pool of blood."

"Sounds excessive."

"We think it was a message. *I'm back and don't fuck with me* sort of thing," said the older of the two.

Dan stood up and stepped towards them. "He's not fucking back. Just because my dad likes having him around as a pet doesn't mean he is part of the family.

I'm still in charge."

"Yeah of course," said the older man "Anyway, we have to brief Bill. Come on," he looked at the younger guy and pushed him towards Bill's office door.

Inside Dan's head, a thousand rats with their fur on fire, were scratching as they tried to get out. His fists were balled like rocks and the rest of his body was tensed, ready to explode.

A small man entered the room from the cellar holding a clipboard and walked up behind him. "Danny boy," he started enthusiastically "looks like you have a stock loss problem. Someone is nicking spirits, Jack Daniels mostly." He finished, pleased he had spotted the problem.

"Who is it?"

"Don't know Danny, but they have done you for nearly a dozen bottles."

Dan erupted. "Your fucking job is to stop this happening not to tell me after someone has robbed us, you fucking moron." Dan dropped the little man with a sucker punch to the gut. As the man went down still holding his clipboard, Dan started kicking him as hard as possible. Desperately the guy tried to keep the board in front of him but several times Dan's foot got through.

Sean entered the club and walked straight towards Bill's door. He glanced over as Dan started again.

"Come on Sean, get stuck in!"

"Even you can handle a little guy like that on your own Dan. Well, probably. Anyway, I don't work for you."

Dan stopped for a second. "You fucking waste of space! Look at me! I'll have you out of here soon!"

Sean carried on as if nothing had happened and

was about to knock on Bill's door when it opened. The two men from the Ford walked out and nodded to him as they passed. Both of them subconsciously give him extra space to avoid an accidental confrontation. He watched them go before he rapped on the wood and walked in.

Behind him, Dan looked down at the bloodied face at his feet. He swung one last kick to the man's head before he began walking away. "And it's not *Danny boy*, it's Mr O`Shea to you, now find out who's stealing our shit."

As Sean entered the room, two faces turned toward him. Bill was seated at his desk and, in the leather chair in front of him, Ray craned his head round to see who had arrived. For a second Sean hesitated. He hadn't expected to see his dad chatting to Bill. Then he realised two brothers talking business was pretty normal.

"How did it go?" asked Bill.

"You already know."

"Sounded like you went a bit over the top," said Ray.

"Just making certain everyone around here gets the message we are not to be fucked with. Sounds like some people are starting to take the piss. That needs to stop."

"What do you..." Bill was cut off by an enormous crash from the bar.

Before the sound had stopped reverberating all three men were bounding towards the door, guns in hand.

As they entered the room all hell had broken loose. Three thugs were beating the snot out of Dan and

Mickey was already lying bleeding on the floor. Bill levelled his gun towards the first one but Sean had already holstered his and dove straight at the guy. The two went down but the Irishman made certain he was back on his feet in a second and drop kicking the other mans head with his right foot. Behind him the second guy swung a chair and caught Sean on the back of the head driving him over a table and out of view.

Bill had also holstered his gun and slid his hand inside a pocket. It came out wrapped through a set of brass knuckles. He immediately started battering the second man who dropped the chair as two solid punches broke his jaw in three places. As he hit the ground Bill stepped over him and was about to start raining more punches down when the sound of a pistol round going supersonic filled the room.

Everyone turned as the third heavy sagged and fell to the floor. The revolver he had been pointing at the back of Bill's head dropped between them.

To his side, Sean kept the gun pointed at the man until he had come to a complete rest and he could see there was no way he would be getting up again. The other two thugs jumped to their feet, ran for the door and burst into the daylight heading for a waiting getaway van.

Sean climbed back on his feet and slid the pistol into its leather holster.

Bill looked at his nephew and then at the huge hole in the dead man's neck.

Sean stood alongside him. "Guess you were right about the cannon shells Bill. They don't get up do they?"

FIVE

Ami Reynolds had lived near the park for 4 years. After she had finally worked up the courage to throw her husband out, it had been one of the few areas she could afford to live in London.

Since she arrived, she had made a deliberate point of avoiding relationships. Olivia ran in front of her heading towards the swings and waved as she passed her mum. Ami mimicked her and shook her hands in the same crazy manner as the six year old. "Love you mum," shouted Olivia.

"Love you more baby," Ami sang back.

Although it was lonely without a man in her life, she thought it was better that Olivia didn't get caught in the middle of a relationship like her old one. One of the advantages of throwing him out was her makeup bills had reduced. No bruises to cover meant she could go more natural and Ami knew she was lucky in that respect. She had always had clear, perfect skin and a creamy complexion. It felt good to not be behind the old mask she was forced to wear.

To her left the gate opened and a big guy walked through with his arms around two young boys. The three of them were laughing uncontrollably like naughty kids.

Ami had seen them several times over the last six months. She guessed he had moved in around here about that time but the boys only appeared every few weeks. "Another single parent," she thought. Maybe he only gets to see them every two weeks. The boys ran over to the swings and instantly started playing with Olivia. Her daughter was younger than them but it was obvious she revelled in being the centre of their attention.

Ami jumped as a voice next to her said "Mind if I sit here?" Somehow the boys dad had made it to her bench without making a sound. He was smiling and pointing to the space beside her.

"No, please feel free," she said. "Are they your sons?"

"Yes, I don't get to see them as often as I would like but this is my weekend. A friend flew down with them for me. Hopefully they will be here full time if things keep going well."

Ami had always been intuitive when it came to peoples feelings. She watched as he spoke. As he talked about them living with him permanently the mans face hardened and became serious. It was obviously important to him and she wondered what their life with their mother was like. Not good she guessed. She liked that the man cared.

"I'm Ami and the little girl flirting with your sons is Olivia."

"Hi Ami, I'm Sean and my boys are Nick and Jim. She certainly has them wound around her little finger. Olivia is very pretty. She is the spitting image of you, I could tell she was your daughter." Sean realised what he had said and flashed a cheeky smile before sitting down beside her.

Ami blushed as the compliment sank in. It was a while since she had received one from someone she liked. For some reason she wasn't intimidated by his size. Instead she felt safe sitting beside the the big man. "Are you local Sean?"

"Yeah, my family are from here and I moved back when I split up with my wife. You?"

"Sort of the same. I moved here after I split with

my husband but I don't have any family here. I chose it because it was cheaper. Nurses salaries won't pay for a penthouse in Mayfair."

"I know what you mean. I got lucky. An old acquaintance did me a favour and found a nice place in the new apartments over there, but it still costs an arm and a leg."

"You must have a good job if you can afford that."

"I work in my uncles family business. He owns 8ish."

"Is your name O'Shea? Sean O'Shea?"

Sean looked at Ami slightly surprised. She was staring at him and looking him up and down as if searching for some clue needed to solve a puzzle.

"You know me?"

"I have heard of you."

Sean could see the concern on her face. "What have you heard about me?"

"That you are dangerous, very dangerous."

"Sorry if that's all you've heard. I am not as bad as the stories and I'm only dangerous to people who are stupid enough to try and cause my family problems." He watched Ami turn away and watch Olivia laughing with Sean's kids."

"You don't seem like the mentalist I hear people talk about. I envisaged Charles Manson instead of a dad looking after his sons. Mind you, Olivia's dad seemed normal up until he punched me in the face."

"Your ex hit you?"

Ami looked at the ground for a second recalling the feel of a fist crushing her cheekbone. "Sometimes."

Seans blood boiled in an instant and his shoulders immediately lifted. He hated men who beat women. Ami looked up and saw his reaction. The tensed muscles, the way his whole body had gone onto alert status. She could see he was ready for action. Even though Ami knew several stories about *Crazy Sean O`Shea,* she still felt safe sitting in his shadow.

Someone beside her said "Would you like to get a coffee?" She looked to her right to see who it was and then realised it was her own voice asking the big man if he would like a drink.

"That would be great. If we go to the little cafe over there, we can sit outside and still watch the kids." Sean stood up and, without thinking, put his arm out.

Ami smiled, stood up and slipped her arm into his.

Sean had spotted the bench as he walked into the park and couldn't help notice the beautiful woman sitting watching the young girl play. It was obvious they were mother and daughter as they both had the same bright blue eyes, blonde hair and matching smiles.

He had spent so much time around the club over the last six months that he had forgotten some women looked stunning wearing no makeup at all. And this girl certainly looked stunning.

Since he had saved Bill's life he had been kept busy. Dan's inability to deal with the Dolan thugs that night had changed the dynamics in the O'Shea family. Sean was now in charge of dealing with the threat from the other East End family and making certain they were kept in their box. Because of this, he had become nocturnal. His day started late afternoon and ran until the club closed at 4am.

The only time that changed was when he had his sons for the weekend. On those days he left the security of the club to his right hand man Geordie.

He had known Geordie for many years and could trust him with his life.

Today was the first time he had experienced daylight in a week and seeing the woman in the bright sunshine made her look even more radiant.

As soon as they entered the park, the boys ran off to play with the little girl on the swings and he decided to see if the seat next to the her mother was free. Unconsciously, he must have been in stealth mode because she jumped as he asked if he could sit down.

As her face turned up towards him he realised she was even more beautiful than he first imagined.

The conversation seemed to flow easily until she realised who he was. For a second he thought he had blown it and she would be repulsed by his violent background, but she seemed ok with it. They had walked to the coffee shop and sat in the sun chatting for over an hour. The conversation never slowed and people walking past assumed they were husband and wife rather than two strangers sharing coffee together.

By the time she had to go they had opened up about their previous marriages, talked about their lives and told each other about their future plans.

For the first time, Sean had felt it unnecessary to be evasive about his life. He decided to just tell her who he was and what he did. Better she know what she was buying if they decided to see each other again. In return, she was completely open with him. Ami talked about the beatings, the reason she decided to stay for so long and how, when she realised enough was enough, she had thrown her worthless husband out.

Ami was the first person Sean had spoken to outside the family in weeks and he really liked her.

Now he was back in the club, he had already started

to wish it was the weekend again so he could call her and arrange to take her out for a drink. Maybe he should invite her to the club? No, not a good idea. Since the incident with the shooting, Dan had become even more deranged. He blamed Sean for everything that went wrong in his life. If he met Ami he would definitely try to fuck up his relationship with her.

Sean walked past the bar. It was full of punters and manned by five members of the staff. He caught the eye of a couple of his team and winked. They smiled back, happy to know he was on the premises. Nothing bad happened when Sean was sheriff for the night.

He saw Bill sitting in a booth talking to another man who was facing away seeming to be deliberately hiding his face. Sean walked over and stood beside the table. "Bill I was wondering if you needed me tonight. I thought I might pop out for a couple of hours." If Bill was ok about it he thought he could phone Ami and see if she could find a sitter for two hours so they could escape for a drink.

"Sorry Sean. It's a big night tonight. I need you on standby."

"No problems. I'll stick around."

He was about to walk away when the other man said "Not going to say hello Sean, you miserable Irish bastard."

"Fuck me! Slippery!" said Sean, genuinely happy to see the old man.

Patrick "Slippery" Shawcross had been part of the O'Shea family for three decades. He was a quiet, well dressed man in his 60's and always looked like he was leaving for a pheasant shoot. His wardrobe looked like the place where tweed went to die.

Slippery was the best brief in the city. More than

once he had kept Sean from enjoying detention at Her Majesty's pleasure. Most cases Patrick became involved with never even made it to a court. Some people believed it was because Slippery had dirt on most of the major players in the justice system, and that was partly true, but mostly it was because he was always the smartest person in the room. He had a knack of making any case seem un-winnable or, at least, massively time consuming to the point that most of them collapsed under their own weight.

"I thought you would be dead by now. There must be a long line of cops wishing you were."

"Sean, you are probably correct but there are a lot more of them terrified if I die, at which point their naughty little lives will become public."

"You devious old git. No wonder no one will touch you."

"You play the cards you get dealt Sean. I don't have the evil streak you do. Old Slippery can't scare them to death like you or Bill so I use the skills I have to swim in the big pond without being eaten."

"Anyone ever gives you any trouble Slippery and you call me. I'll make certain they decide to take an indefinite holiday from the human race. I still owe you. I wouldn't have seen my kids grow up if it wasn't for you."

"Thank you Sean, it's nice to know my services have done some good, but all that has been paid for a long time ago by your uncle. There is no debt."

Sean looked and Bill nodded. "And I am very grateful to my uncle but I still have a debt of honour with you Patrick."

Slippery nodded acceptance but Sean only turned and left when he was certain the old guy was clear he was serious.

"He's a good lad Bill," said Slippery. "Not many like him nowadays."

Bill watched Sean walk away. "No, there aren't Slippery. He is very special to me. A good man. Glad he's back where he belongs."

Bill and Patrick watched the big guy walk towards the bar as a young dark skinned girl stepped in front of him. They spoke a few words and then she slapped Sean in the face so hard that it forced him back on his heels.

"Looks like he has a way with the ladies as well," said Slippery with a smirk on his face. "Just like his dad."

Bill looked over at his brother. Ray was at the end of the bar chatting to a waitress."

"Yeah, just like his dad, the O'Sheas always make the bad decisions when it comes to women."

Sean was pleased he had seen Slippery. For a long time he had wanted to thank him in person for the help he had given him. Without Patrick, he would be seeing his sons on visiting days only and that's if their tart of a mother decided to bring them to the prison.

He walked back to the bar to check in with Geordie and find out if there was anything he needed to deal with urgently. Sean knew there wouldn't be, Geordie was a safe pair of hands and managed things as if he was the boss.

Fifteen feet away from the bar, a petite young woman stepped in front of him. She was beautiful, obviously mixed race and she held her head high as if the world held no worries for her. Underneath the confident exterior, she wore a tired expression and years of living with a drug user told him her body was under the stress of some heavy chemical compounds.

"Sean O'Shea?" she said.

"Yes sweetheart, how can I help," Sean met her with a welcoming grin on his face. He looked past her and caught Geordie's eye for a second. As he glanced down again he was too late spotting the roundhouse slap to the face that was only inches away from his cheek. The crack it made was so loud everyone within 30 feet stopped dead in their tracks.

"You bastard!"

Sean picked her up like she weighed nothing. As he threw her over his shoulder she began screaming at the top of her voice "Help me! Stop you pig!"

No-one moved a muscle. They all thought it was better not to get involved in Sean's business.

At the fire exit he kicked the door open and walked into the alley beside the club. The girl was kicking the air and punching his back but it made no impact at all to the big Irishman's trajectory. At the curb he dropped her to the ground but made certain she didn't fall as her feet touched down.

"Goodnight miss, time to go home and clean yourself up." Sean turned back to the door and grabbed the handle.

"Call yourself a dad."

He stopped in mid stride. "Did Jean send you?"

The look on the girls face was the same as if he had slapped her. The hurt expression quickly changed back to anger again and she spat at his face and then ran into the main street.

"When did my life turn into Alice in fucking Wonderland. I can't remember falling down a pissing rabbit hole." His words echoed off the brick wall on the other side of the alley.

"Fuck it!" he said and walked back into the club.

Around the corner, Tasha collapsed back against the wall. She slid down and wrapped her arms around her legs sobbing in deep gulping breaths.

A voice above her asked "So how did that work out for you?" Karl was nervously looking in either direction as he spoke. Tasha looked up as he pulled a hand out of his pocket. Between his fingers was a small clear ziplock baggie with white powder inside.

"Pick me up?" he said.

She smiled, stood up and grabbed it out of his hand. "Thank you darling," she said as she kissed him. They walked across the street, turned left and disappeared into the darkness.

Bill was waiting at the bar when Sean walked back in. Slippery had left and his uncle looked like he wanted a quiet word.

"What the fuck was that about Bill? Whoever she is she's barred."

"Tasha came around here a year ago looking for you. I keep an eye on her from time to time but she hasn't been back in months."

"Why are you keeping an eye on her? She's a nutball. Anyway she won't be allowed in here again."

"You cannot bar her."

"I can bar anyone I like Bill as long as I'm responsible for this place running smoothly."

"O'Sheas don't bar family."

"What? Which fuck-wit in the family is she related to?"

"You, you daft twat. Tasha is Donna's daughter…
…and yours."

SIX

The club was at capacity and the noise was deafening. A mixture of music and well oiled voices combined to create a constant drone that drowned out all but the loudest conversations.

Although the public were still allowed in, Bill was hosting his wife's birthday in the club at the same time. The two had been married for nearly four decades and June was the perfect gangland wife. Tough, supportive and silent. Over the years she had seen her fair share of the family's business and even though Bill had tried to keep her away from the messier episodes, some things were impossible to avoid. In all that time, she hadn't spoken a word about what she had seen. Not even with the other O'Sheas. Bill knew he had a diamond and made certain she was treated accordingly. Tonight was a no expense spared event and all the members of their extended family were invited. By 9:30pm they had all made good use of the free bar Bill had provided and the evening was in full swing.

Sean walked through the crowd with a head full of conflicting thoughts. When Bill had told him about Tasha and that his old girlfriend had decided to hide her pregnancy from the family, it started to make sense of Donna's abrupt end to their relationship. She was a stunning young woman, the direct result of amazing Afro Caribbean genes. Donna never really came to terms with his family connections, especially as their relationship was directly in the middle of the IRA attacks on London. Sean hadn't realised how much he had fallen for her until the day she abruptly ended it all.

For a couple of years he threw himself into the

business and a steady string of meaningless relationships until he eventually met Jean. Within a couple of months she had worked her way into his life and the rest was history.

What Sean couldn't work out was why Bill hadn't told him when Tasha turned up at the club a year ago looking for her dad. Somewhere along the line, Tasha had become very angry and obviously blamed Sean for something.

He needed some air and a bit of quiet to think. As he walked to the main entrance, Dan was heading in the opposite direction. "Did I miss the fun earlier? I really wanted to be around when you met Tasha. Nice piece of arse isn't she? Did Sean get all upset? Diddums!."

"Fuck you Dan. Best you get back in your box before I put you in one. I'm not in the mood tonight so you better keep your distance and shut that fucking ugly mouth." The sentence finished abruptly and Dan knew the words missing were "Or else." He decided he would have more fun behind the scenes and not to push the point, especially in Seans current mood.

The two carried on walking in opposite directions. At the main door Sean stepped into the night and took a deep breath. Geordie was on the door and raised his eyebrows in a silent exchange that said *are you ok*?

He nodded back to Geordie and forced out a small smile. Sean looked right at the long line of people already waiting to get into the club. In the distance, Karl exchanged something with a guy waiting in line. Sean looked back at Geordie who had also seen it and was dispatching a bouncer to fix the problem. As the big guy caught up with Karl he placed a high hand in his chest and shoved firmly. The result was Karl ending up in the street sitting on his arse. He looked angrily at Sean, climbed to his feet and shuffled away trying to hide his embarrassment.

As Sean started to turn back to Geordie and say "good job" he spotted Ami standing in the queue with four friends. She looked stunning in a short black dress and matching heels. When they had shared a coffee a few days earlier he had the impression her body was very toned but had no idea how amazing it looked when more of her skin was on show.

"Geordie, see the blonde in the black dress?"

"No Sean, I definitely didn't notice the slim, perky blue eyed girl with the killer legs and the amazing arse. I was too busy giving my guide dog a biscuit."

"Funny Geordie, very fucking funny. While I wait for tickets to your one man stand up show, could you make yourself useful, pull Ami's party out of line and escort them to the VIP booths?"

"No problem boss," said Geordie. "It will be a pleasure." He lit up with his best cheeky Chappy smile and wandered over.

"Good evening ladies, Ami isn't it?" he said in a heavy Newcastle accent. Ami nodded and looked past Geordie towards where Sean had been standing. He had disappeared back inside. "Just to let you know your VIP booth is ready now and you should follow me." The girls all looked at Ami and started giggling as they followed Geordie back towards the doors.

As they walked along the queue a couple of lads, who had been waiting a while, looked less than happy the girls had dodged the line. "Guess a pair of tits gets you immediate entry to this place."

Geordie stopped, walked back to the guy who had just shot his mouth off and leant into his face. "I'm staring at a pair of tits and that hasn't helped you get in has it?"

The lads looked in different directions as Geordie glowered at them. He returned to the ladies, switched back into gracious host mode, and walked them to the booths on the mezzanine. As the girls sat down Ami said she would order drinks at the bar and wandered through the crowd. As she made it to the front of the line a voice close to her ear made her jump. "Having a good time?"

As she turned Seans lips were so close they brushed her skin. As he leaned back as a warm shiver ran down her neck. It was a long time since her body had had that type of reaction around a man.

"Yes! Thank you for letting us in so quickly, I was starting to get cold." Sean's large hands clasped hers and the heat flowed through her fingers. For a few seconds they just stared before Sean broke the moment.

"Go sit down, I'll send drinks over for you."

"How do you know what we like?"

"If I get it wrong I'll buy you dinner Monday. If I get it right you can take me out instead."

"Sneaky," she said. "I like your enthusiasm though." Ami walked back to the table and a few minutes later two bottles of Louis Roederer turned up at the table along with six glasses.

"Thanks," Ami said to the waitress "but we only need five."

"Don't I get to have a glass of my own Champagne?" Sean slid in beside her.

"Of course," she said enjoying feeling his leg pressed up against hers.

Her friends clinked glasses and said thanks for the

drinks.

"Aren't you going to say thank you too Ami," her friends giggled.

Ami leant forward, slid her arms around his neck and pulled him in. As their lips touched, the same shiver ran down her neck and this time didn't stop at her shoulders. The girls clapped and shouted as the two kissed, but as far as Sean was concerned there wasn't another person in the room apart from Ami.

Eventually they parted and he stepped back. "I need to check a few things around the club."

As she watched him walk away one of her friends leant close. "You are too eager Ami, make him work a bit."

"I really like him."

"Then you are going to have to do something about your husband. This will never end well."

Five miles away Mickey was picking up the slack Dan had left in the business. Since Sean had returned, Dan had become more distant from the day to day running of the family's operations. Instead, he spent most of his time working out ways he could piss his cousin off. Mickey was getting sick of it. Beyond the amount of work he was having to do, he had become a pingpong ball between the two of them. He had always liked Sean, even when they were kids. More so than his brother. His dad treated the three of them the same so, to Mickey, it felt as if he had two older brothers not just one. It didn't matter to him that Bill welcomed Sean into the close family. Quite the opposite. Bill was getting older. Once he was a huge powerhouse of a man that no-one would ever cross but, in recent years, his age had started catching up with him and other crews had started taking liberties. That was until Sean came back. Now everyone was treating the O'Sheas like royalty again. Well, except for the Dolans. The bad blood ran too deep between the families and they still coveted the smuggling and door security sides of the business. It had always been a badge of honour which business supplied the doormen in the big West End clubs and casinos. For twenty years that had been the O'Sheas.

Mickey shouted orders to the three man team loading a large anonymous truck. As soon as this lot was on board he could head to the club and relax for the evening to celebrate his mums birthday.

The shutters behind him rattled slightly. Mickey walked over to a door on the left which was set into the main panel. He opened the catch and stuck his head through. As soon as it cleared the frame a fist holding a Glock smashed him in the mouth. The lights didn't go out but he lay on the floor dazed and bleeding. Above him stood the two men who had attacked the club a few months before.

"Get up," said the one closest to him. "We have a message for your dad."

As Mickey pulled himself to his feet, several men ran past him into the warehouse and each was carrying some type of hand cannon.

"Times have changed boy. Your family have just been put on notice that their world has come to an end."

He dragged Mickey over to his car. "Now, fuck off and tell Bill his doormen services won't be needed tomorrow night. Our boys will be taking over the West End, now piss off."

Mickey fished his keys out of his pocket, started the

engine and accelerated towards Soho.

June was having a great evening. Bill had handed her the keys to a new Range Rover to replace the previous one that was still only months old. She had mentioned she had seen a pretty white version a few weeks ago and Bill had made certain she had whatever she wanted to be happy. In the box with the gift wrapped keys was a bracelet covered in diamonds. It made a little circle around the keys themselves.

As much as she loved the presents, what she enjoyed more was the fact that her family were together. She was standing at the bar surrounded by Dan, Ray, Sean and Bill. As soon as Mickey arrived the O'Shea men would be complete. They had spent ten minutes showering her with compliments and handing over gifts. June's life was perfect.

In the distance, Bills elder sister, Sean's aunt May, returned from the toilet. The poor old love had become confused in the last few years and had started struggling to remember who was who. She barged through the men and stopped in front of Bill's wife. "June darling, can you ask one of these waiters to get me a stout. They have been standing around doing nothing all evening, the lazy little Gob shite's." Her heavy Irish accent had travelled with her to England fifty years earlier and time had not softened it.

"They aren't waiters May, it's the boys, ours and Rays lad."

She looked around the group inspecting them in more detail. "As I said darling, useless Gob shite's, now get me a stout or do I have to do it myself?" Without waiting she stomped back to her table. As she left they noticed her skirt was tucked in her knickers along with several sheets of toilet roll.

June scuttled after her to save her from embarrassment.

Dan and Sean burst out laughing.

"Oi you two! She's confused now shut the fuck up."

Ray suddenly became distracted and left the group as he saw Mickey enter through a side door. He met his nephew halfway across the room and started an animated conversion. Oblivious to this, Sean had wandered back to Ami's table and sipped his glass of Champagne as he chatted with her."

Ray appeared beside him. "We have a problem."

His son had tuned out the world around him and was concentrating on the woman in front of him.

"Hey!" shouted Ray.

Sean turned and Ray nodded towards Mickey. He could see a small trail of blood from a split lip. "Sorry ladies, I need to sort a few things out for a minute. Keep enjoying the evening and order what drinks you like." Ray walked behind him and on the way they spotted Tasha with Karl's arm wrapped around her waist. Sean started to step sideways, changing his destination but Ray grabbed his arm. "Keep focussed, this is important." He allowed his dad to steer him until he had joined Mickey and the rest of the group. On mass they headed towards Bill's office and closed the door as soon as they were all inside.

"So what's going on?" Said Bill.

"It's the Dolans, dad. They turned up at the warehouse. I was sent back with a message. They said the smuggling business was theirs now, and the door business up west."

"Fuckers are deluded if they think they can turn up and we will just roll on our backs with our legs in the air," said Bill looking at Sean.

He nodded. "This has to be dealt with tonight Bill."

Dan stood at the back and realised his dad expected his cousin to fix the problem. His blood boiled and he stepped through the bodies until he was in front of Bill. "Don't fuck around. Send a proper message, like old times. A little present under their car in the morning will remind them who they are dealing with."

"We don't do that anymore. The last thing we need is the domestic terrorist team looking us over," said Sean.

Dan stepped up to his cousins face. "You might not have the bottle to do it but I'm still an O'Shea. I say blow the fuckers up!"

"You're a mentalist Dan. What, we end up with a load of collateral damage? All we need is a kid being blown to pieces and the Gavvers will never leave us alone. A thousand Slippery's wouldn't be able to get us off. No, better to handle it the old way. We'll go down there and do the bastards. Bill, open the safe."

His uncle walked to the back wall and thumbed a catch. A panel popped open and behind it a massive gun case sat hidden behind the wall. The combination spun as Bill rotated it backwards and forwards. A loud click signalled the lock had released so he turned the handle and swung the steel door wide.

Each man stepped forward and picked up a gun as well as a few spare magazines.

As soon as they were all tooled up they used the rear door to access the side street and the cars parked there.

As the last men left, Dan had held back, he grabbed Mickey by the arm. "I still say an incendiary is what is needed."

"Come on Dan, that's a bit strong."

Mickey followed him through the door and rolled his eyes as he came level with one of their old time heavies. Tommy nodded and closed the exit behind them.

The line of four black Range Rovers had stopped at the entrance to the main road leading to the warehouse. Each man slid on a dark grey, one piece coverall and gloves. The last thing any of them needed was to end up covered in gunshot residue. That would hand the old bill exactly what they needed if someone was picked up later. They climbed back in the cars and accelerated through the doors of the warehouse. Four sets of headlights on main beam picked out a dozen Dolan heavies. Sean piled out of the lead car and began blazing away. As the man who had blindsided Mickey opened his mouth a bullet caught him squarely in the cheek and flipped him onto his back. He lay on the concrete, blood oozing out of the hole where his ear used to be.

Behind him, the rest of the team followed suit and a hail of bullets cut six of the guys down before one shot could be returned.

Fifteen feet behind Sean, Dan emerged from the last vehicle and began unloading into the crates a few of of the Dolan's were using as cover. The wood seemed solid and a safe place for them to shelter behind, but a 9mm at short distance tears through it like butter. Two bullets left Dan's gun a split second apart and both punched through the wall of a crate and the man crouching behind it.

Sean was right in front of him now. Dan realised a

lot could be hidden in a shootout this chaotic. He lifted his gun and levelled it at the back of Sean's head. As he increased pressure on the trigger he caught sight of Mickey watching him with his jaw hanging open. Dan instantly swung the gun and fired three rounds towards the last of the heavies.

Within two minutes the room was silent.

One minute later they were back in the cars and fifteen after that back at the Club. In total, they had been away for less than an hour. In Bill's office the men stripped off the coveralls, lost the gloves and dumped it all in a huge sack along with the guns.

Sean stuck his head out of the door and waved at Geordie. As he approached he said "Yes boss?"

"Cut the *yes boss* shit Geordie. I need you to work fast. Out through the back. Take this sack and three men with you. I want this destroyed and all the cars torched by midnight. Understand?"

"It's done Sean." Geordie was gone in an instant.

In the club, the music was abruptly cut and the room fell silent.

Bill's door opened and all the O'Sheas walked into the room. At the front Bill carried a huge cake complete with lit candles. As they marched towards June's table they started a chorus of happy birthday and everyone in the room joined in. Sean could see Ami and the girls singing along in the distance.

June had tears in her eyes as they surrounded her and finished in a crescendo.

"Happy birthday baby," said Bill and kissed his wife. The whole room erupted into cheers and the music started again.

Sean walked over to Ami's table and grabbed her by the hand. She thought he was taking her for a dance but he ducked through the cellar door and pushed it shut behind them. "I'm fed up with sharing you with a room full of people," he said and pulled her into his arms.

"Works for me," she said and reached up for the kiss. Three glasses of Champagne, a year being celibate and the excitement of finding a man she could fall in love with exploded inside her. After the initial touch of their lips subsided she pushed hard on his chest and broke away. He thought he had gone too far and she was rejecting him.

"Sean O'Shea, you are about to be luckiest man on earth. Ami pulled at the zip running down the entire back of her dress. It fell to the ground and she stepped back into his arms.

Even after the evenings events, it was only now his mouth went dry and he was lost for words.

"Come on big boy, lets see if you are as dangerous with those hands as I have heard."

Twenty minutes later they emerged, still trying to straighten their clothes. Ami headed straight to the toilet to replace the lipstick she had lost, Sean headed for the gents to remove all the lipstick he had gained.

They emerged at the same time, grinning like teenagers as they met back at her booth. He caught one of her friends mouthing the words "what the fuck?" to Ami as she straightened her dress.

She blushed and shrugged. Sean liked the way she was self conscious enough to have her cheeks colour but confident enough to take the lead and initiate the next stage of their relationship.

"I'll get another bottle ladies if that's ok?" Sean headed over to one of the waitress and leant in to give her specific instructions. As he finished Dan stepped up beside him. "Having fun?"

"What do you mean Dan? It's been a busy evening thanks to you not taking care of the business for so long and I'm not in the mood."

Dan's heckles raised but then he decided there was a better way to bait Sean. "She is a nice piece of arse old man. I'd pay for a piece of that any day. Do me a favour and see if you can get mates rates. Fuck it, I'd pay maybe ten quid for a blow job from her. Of course she would have to swallow for that."

Before Dan had finished the last syllable his throat was crushed by Sean's huge fist. His head was smashed against the wall behind him and his cousin reached into his jacket for a gun that wasn't there. As it came out empty Sean spun Dan around and locked a grip around his neck and began choking him out.

Across the room, Tasha staggered out of the toilets, stoned, high and swaying.

Sean looked at the bar and Geordie. His friend had been watching the confrontation as he arrived back at the club. Dan sagged as his brain was starved of oxygen. Just before he passed out, the big mans grip released. Sean nodded towards his cousin who was now lying at his feet. The look *said get him into the office before he ends up dead*. Geordie summoned another bouncer and the two of them carried Dan into Bill's office.

Tasha was holding a wall trying to stay on her feet and a random guy was rubbing her arse as she struggled to focus. Her dad stormed over, dropped the man with a single punch to his guts and held her upright. Immediately two heavies picked the man up and dragged him to the fire exit. The only people who noticed what had happened was a barman and a waitress. He turned back to Tasha. "What going on? Why are you doing this to yourself? You know I didn't…"

"Fuck off you bastard. I'm just having fun, just like you and your tart!" She pulled away and a rush of adrenalin kicked in. It gave her the strength to stumble into the crowd.

Before he could catch up with Tasha, Mickey grabbed his arm and pulled him back towards the family. "Mum's big surprise is about to go on stage. You are expected to be with us."

Sean looked into the crowd but Tasha was gone. He allowed himself to be escorted over to the O'Shea birthday party.

"She's going to love this," said Bill. "June has always liked Jim Wilson."

Sean looked confused. "Jim Wilson?"

"You know, the little bloke with the squeaky voice. Tells fruity jokes, comes over a bit gay," said Bill.

"The little bloke with the squeaky voice? Bill, Jim Wilson is the guy on YouTube who has a beard. He Fs and Blinds all the time?"

"Don't be a cock Sean. Tonights not the night to wind me up."

The music died and Bill walked towards the small stage.

"Er Bill," shouted Sean. "The little guy is Jim Walton. I think you may have made a monumental balls-up."

Sean was drowned out by thunderous applause as Bill made it to the microphone.

"Ladies, Gentlemen and my beautiful wife June. As a special surprise we have invited a guest who is here to entertain us. He's my wife's favourite comedian, a British legend, please put your hands together for Jim!"

As the cheers erupted a bearded hippy wearing a sexy leprechauns outfit, complete with green stockings and suspenders, walked on stage carrying a pint of Guinness.

June looked at aunt May, then at the shambling tramp in the green mini dress and back to aunt May. "Jim Walton has grown a beard, put on weight and started cross dressing. I think he has let himself go May?"

"Evening," said Wilson taking a huge gulp out of his pint. "Is this the right place for the Irish birthday party? I fucking hope so or I've wasted fifty quid in the Ann Summers St Patrick's Day section. Mind you, I did get a free vibrator… …so… …good deal really."

June looked at Bill with a big frown growing across her face. Bill looked at the comedian and then back at June. He wasn't a panicky man but he could feel sweat forming under his arms.

On stage, Wilson took another gulp, finished his pint and lifted a new one out of a pocket in his skirt. "You might be impressed with that bit of magic but you would be more amazed if you knew where I'm hiding the vibrator right now. Let's just say I'm buzzing tonight," and he took another big swig of Guinness as he rubbed his arse.

Sean made his way back to Ami, laughing so hard he was crying.

"What's so funny?" said Ami.

"See that old man over there? The one with sweat all over his forehead?"

"Yeah."

"Well you are about to watch the oldest dog in the kennel get castrated."

June walked over to Bill and started waving her hands, pointing at the comedian and shouting at her husband.

Just as she started twirling her arms like the sails of a deranged windmill, the doors burst open and a dozen police marched into the room.

June walked straight over to the group and said "Come with me, he's over here."

D.I. Holmes, striding ahead of the group, had his arm grabbed and he began being dragged towards the stage. He was used to taking charge of situations and was expecting a fight when it came to arresting the O'Shea family. What he wasn't expecting was a small, angry, blonde lady to start ordering his officers around as if they worked for her.

"Well don't just stand there, come with me. He's not getting money out of us for this." June pushed two of the largest officers towards the stage. "Him, he's here under false pretences."

Jim Wilson was used to dealing with hecklers, but not ones that turned up mob handed with police in tow. "What? What is she on about?"

"You're not getting paid," said June. She turned to the officers. "He's pretending to be Jim Walton and not doing a very good job."

"I'm not Jim Walton," said Wilson.

"See, he admits it. Go on, lock him up."

D.I. Holmes had been watching from a distance, unable to understand how a raid had gone so wrong, so quickly. He stepped between June and his officers to settle things down. "Look I think you have made a mistake. We are not here to arrest him," he tried to explain.

June pushed Holmes towards the stage but he caught his shoe on a cable and lost his footing. The detective stumbled backwards and fell onto the stage. The other uniforms sprang into action. Two of them grabbed her arms and pinned her to the spot as the others tried to pick up their boss. Sean had been standing close by. As June became the focus of everyones attention, most of the O'Shea mob, including Dan, had slipped out of the exits. Sean was happy to allow them the chance to get away but now his aunt was being manhandled by the police he needed to calm things down. He took hold of the restraining officers arms as he separated June from their grasp. One of them tried to maintain his grip but Sean pulled his arm back to get it away from his aunt. As he tugged the uniform, he lost his grip and his elbow flew backwards. Unfortunately, Holmes was just getting back on his feet and Sean's arm caught him under the chin and sent him flying again. At this point the situation went sideways. A truncheon caught the Irishman on the back of the head, fists started flying and everyone else made a dash for the door.

At that point a pile of men landed on Sean and cuffs clicked onto his wrists behind his back.

Jim Wilson stood on stage watching the brawl as the room descended into chaos. He decided the chances of being paid were somewhere south of nil. Better to get out now than push the point.

"Thank you for being a great audience," he said. "and just remember, if you have any comments please leave them on Facebook. My names Jim Walton. Good-night!" As he walked off dodging the riot, he mumbled to himself, "They wanted Walton they can complain about Walton".

SEVEN

D.I. Holmes clicked the record button on the desk top tape machine. "D.I. Holmes interviewing Sean O'Shea in regards to the murder of several members of the Dolan gang in a shootout on the evening of 14th July at approximately 10pm. In attendance: myself, Sean O'Shea and his legal representative Mr Patrick Shawcross. O'Shea, you might as well tell us why you did it. Your family isn't getting off this time. The best thing you can hope for is coming clean to reduce your sentence."

"Mr," said Slippery.

"Mr What?," said Holmes.

"It's Mr O'Shea. He hasn't been charged and should therefore be treated as a member of the public helping with police enquiries."

Holmes stared at both of them. "I don't give a shit what you want to be called. Everyone knows your family are all slags and most are ex IRA. Don't piss me off or any deal you might want to make is gone."

Sean looked at Slippery "Can you smell bacon?" Patrick started to laugh.

"You two are a couple of funny fuckers aren't you?"

"D.I. Holmes," said Slippery "My client is just speculating that their may be some breakfast being prepared, he hasn't eaten since yesterday. Perhaps a bacon sandwich and some tea?"

"Don't push your luck O'Shea, you better start talking or your nuts will end up in my trophy case."

Sean leaned onto the desk and growled into Holmes face. "Luck is not a factor you useless fucking flatfoot." He sat back and nodded to Slippery.

"Holmes," said Patrick deliberately not using his title "I think you should read this before you slander a leading businessman in the local community." He pushed two pages across the table. Holmes looked down and read the title. "Signed Statement of Ami Reynolds. 14th July." He looked at the brief and said "What is this shit?"

"This Holmes, is a signed statement from Mr O'Shea's girlfriend to say that she was with him all evening from 8:30 until your officers barged into a private party. In fact there are another fifty people who will testify to the same."

"Bollocks! I know you and your mob had a shootout with the Dolans at one of your warehouses last night."

Sean crossed his arms and smiled, "We don't have any warehouses. Now, can I go or do you want to wank yourself dry, fantasising over arresting me?"

Holmes jumped to his feet. "Listen you fucking piece of shit."

Sean stood up towering over him. "Sit down now or let me go before the little dog gets fucked by the big dog."

"You're in my kennel you bog hopping Irish shit."

Just as the two started to square off a knock on the door stopped the confrontation. A head popped around the corner and a WPC looked into the room. "What the fuck do you want?" he said.

She panicked and said "The results of the GSR tests came back. They are negative."

Sean looked at Slippery and raised his eyebrows. Patrick leaned close and said "GSR is *Gunshot residue*. Apparently you haven't fired a gun at all. Isn't that the case Holmes?"

The Detective scowled at the WPC and then turned back to his detainee. "It doesn't change a thing. We have witnesses."

"That you may Detective. I just hope they are not members of the criminal enterprise known as the Dolan gang. That would be a conflict of interest on their part and a motive for their perjured testimony," said Slippery "I hope for the sake of your case my client's accusers don't test positive for GSR." Everyone looked towards the PC standing in the doorway. She looked embarrassed and then walked out and closed the door.

"Oh dear Holmes. Looks like Watson has pissed on your parade." Slippery got up and beckoned to Sean as he headed for the exit. "We'll be going now unless you have anything else to say. Well, apart from the apology for wasting Mr O'Shea's time."

Holmes switched off the recorder as Sean followed Patrick. Just before he walked out of the room he said. "Be seeing you, you fucking prick."

"Smile now but I've got one of your family next door and he really wants to talk about you. Seems he thinks you are a nasty bastard and should be put away. See you soon O'Shea."

Patrick stopped outside the door. "You get out, I've got to deal with Dan. He's starting to get pissed off and may start talking."

"I thought he got out?"

"He did, but he's so stupid he went straight home and the police were waiting for him. He's not like you Sean. He is messed up in the head and you returning has pushed him over the edge. Don't worry, I'll fix it."

Slippery knocked on the interview room door next to the one Sean had just left. He walked in and just before the door closed, the Irishman heard Slippery say "Hello Dan, what have you bolloxed up now my boy?"

Sean stepped up to the desk and picked up his personal belongings. Sitting in the waiting room was one of the Dolan's cousins. As O'Shea walked out through the main doors he stepped up to the desk. "How come my family are still in custody and that Irish bastard has walked free?"

"Three reasons. First he has Slippery Shawcross as his brief. Second you aren't IRA. Third, and most important, he isn't a stupid twat that grasses up his people like your family do. Now fuck off before I stick you in a cell for being an ugly cock."

The Dolan watched Sean walk away and decided to sit quietly until he could bail out the others.

In the second interview room Dan was ranting at the top of his voice. "Why did you nick me? It's Sean, my cousin, not me! He is the boss! I just work at the club."

Patrick put his hand on Dan's arm. "My client is obviously under some sort of duress and doesn't know what he is talking about. I insist on ending this interview immediately until I can have a chance to speak to my client on his own."

Holmes sensed Dan's need to kick his cousin while he was down. He definitely didn't want Slippery talking to him alone right now. "I don't think that is necessary. Tell me more about it Dan. How is your cousin involved in these deaths and how did he get an alibi for last night?"

Dan opened his mouth but Patrick stood up and said "End it now!" He looked down at Dan who wiped the smile off his face as Holmes left the room.

"Dan," said Slippery "We need to have a conversation before your big fucking mouth gets you killed darling."

The cafe was half empty. It hadn't changed in thirty years. Partly because the locals liked it to remain like a little time capsule in the middle of their community but, mostly, because Bill owned it and didn't want another Starbucks where he couldn't get a decent mug of tea.

The booth in the corner always had a reserved sign on the table. That's where the old man knew he would have a seat with its back to the wall.

Slippery walked though the door and straight over to where Bill was waiting. As he sat down he spotted the black coffee ready for him at his seat. "We know each other too well don't we Bill." Patrick sat down and looked at his old friend who smiled up at him. "Look, I know Dan has never really liked Sean for whatever reason, but he's going too far, it's like he has a fixation with him."

"What happened?" said Bill.

"You need to end this now. Talk to the pair of them. Dan would have laid every single crime on Sean this morning, if I hadn't shut him up. The police desperately wanted to hear more."

"Bloody idiot. He's always been jealous. Always has been."

Bill, this needs to be fixed. I'm not a genius and the police aren't stupid. They will lean on Dan and find out more if it's not sorted. They already smell a rat and Dan is a bloody liability at the moment."

"Leave it with me. Meet me at 8ish in the club and

I'll have some answers tonight."

"Good, but let me be clear. If you don't, you could all end up behind bars for the rest of your lives."

Ami's house was a shit-hole. But it was a well maintained shit-hole. When Sean had first moved back he had rented a place near the park her child played in. It was the only place he could afford locally that had enough bedrooms for him and his sons. Now he saw Ami's, he realised how lucky he was. Sometimes it pays to have people who can do you a favour. As he sat in the Range Rover and stared at her house. The thought that she had to walk around these streets on her own kicked in 100,000 years of instincts which were hard coded into his DNA. He needed to protect her and she had to escape this place. Ami had shown she was quite capable of looking after herself but when something is part of your basic nature you can't ignore the voices that start talking to your subconscious.

His phone lit up and a person's name appeared on the screen. As he lifted the mobile he pressed the accept button. "Yeah! Sure! You been ok since I picked you up at the airport? Good. See you later, Serj. Cheers!"

He stepped out of the car and walked down the tiny path to Ami's door. As he knocked he saw a shadow walk past part of the frosted glass. Two catches clicked and it swung wide. Ami stood in front of him wearing a pair of Pilates pants and a matching T-shirt. She looked amazing, if a little tired.

"God, Sean! I was so worried. Some solicitor asked me to sign a statement. He said it would help you. How did you know where I live?"

"Slippery found your address. He's good at that. Thanks for your help, I owe you."

"Slippery?" she said and then the penny dropped. The name fitted the lawyer perfectly. Suddenly her body language changed. She tipped her head and looked past him and into the distance with a concerned expression on her face. "Look, it's difficult at the moment Sean, you can't stay here, talking. I'll pop over and see you at the club later.

"What's the problem, Ami?"

"Please, just go, I'll see you tonight."

"Ok but I still owe you. Can I take you for dinner?"

"Let's discuss it at the club."

"Ok." Sean stepped back and walked down the path. As he was about to step onto the street a man stood in front of him. Momentarily the two locked gazes. Twenty years ago, Sean had stood in a ring with men like this. When you are not wearing gloves the world becomes crystal clear. He had read faces like this in the past and knew the man was one step away from throwing a punch. He only had two options, hit him first or back him down. He chose the latter. The big Irishman stood his ground and filled the path. "Have you got a problem or do you want one?"

In a second, the mans self preservation instincts cut in and he lowered his eyes and stepped aside.

Sean looked back as the guy reached the door and pulled a key out of his pocket. As it slid into the lock he pushed it wide and then slammed it behind him.

For a second, Sean started walking back but he remembered Ami asking him to leave. He could talk to her later and clear this up, but every fibre in his body screamed, "Storm back into the house right now."

In the last twenty years his instincts had served him

well but now he decided that it was time to give others their chance to exercise theirs. He just hoped he wasn't wrong.

"I've had enough of Sean, he's pissing me off now. Dad's always siding with him. It's like Sean is part of the family and I'm not," Dan looked up and realised what he had said. " I mean, we aren't."

Mickey looked at his brother. "I don't know why it bothers you, it doesn't bother me. Sean was always good to me and we are all the same blood." He saw Dan's face cloud and his shoulders raise. For a second it was like seeing a dog turn on it's owner.

"I'm going to have him Mickey, I will rip his guts out!"

"Seriously Dan, what's your problem? You were both my big brothers when we were kids. I don't get this shit you give him."

Dan spun his head so they were eye to eye. "He… …is… …not… …your… …brother, and if you think he is, you're not mine!"

"Fuck me, is it that important? Sean is keeping the Dolan's in their kennel. Dad is not the man he was and our cousin has filled the gap. Why can't you accept it."

"Because he left us and abandoned the family. He gave up being an O'Shea. Now he is just staff and dad must see that. I should be in command and telling the hired help what to do," Dan looked at Mickey "I meant we should be telling them what to do."

"Dan, you are a piece of shit but you are still my brother so I need to say this to you. I may not be the eldest in the family but I can still tell you that you are going to fuck us all if you don't grow some balls and get past this. Accept Sean and we can all begin to regrow the business. Don't start a family feud. It will only help the Dolans."

"Mickey, when all this crap settles down, you best be in a position where I can throw you a bone. Don't pick the wrong side."

"I didn't realise we had sides in the family Dan." Mickey walked away. He hoped he wouldn't be put in a position where he had to choose between his brother or his cousin. It wasn't a place that anyone who knew them would want to be.

Maddy had been trying to get a job at the club for nearly a year. It was *the* place to be seen in London and a perfect place to accelerate her modelling career. Some of the most influential people in the world passed through its doors. One of her friends had picked up her first modelling contract here and another had been discovered by a film director. Even a barman had made it into several television adverts.

Hopefully lightning would strike her as well.

As she entered the club, the night air had cooled her skin and she was showing a lot. It was important that she made a good impression on her first night because she would be on probation indefinitely. Maddy knew the first problem the management had with her would be the last, and there was a long, long queue of people who wanted her job.

As she entered the club it was still in the process of setting up for that evenings opening. A few staff were restocking shelves and wiping down tables. Leaning against the bar was a big man handing out orders as he walked around the room. Maddy knew him from several nights drinking in 8ish. His name was

Sean and everyone knew at least one story about him. She looked him over. Not a bad looking man. It wouldn't hurt to get to know him. In fact, it might be quite fun. She walked over to him and held out her hand. "Hi Mr O'Shea, I'm Maddy."

Sean looked down at the bubbly young woman in front of him. "Hello treacle, you look very happy."

"I am, I've got the job I have wanted for ages. I'm your new barmaid."

"Lovely to have you as part of the team. You'll enjoy it. We treat people well here and everyone gets on with each other. If they don't, they never last long."

"Do you think I will fit in around here?," said Maddy stepping slightly closer.

Sean smiled down at her as she popped her hands on her hips and and stared up through her enormous false eyelashes.

"I think you will go down a storm babe."

In the distance Ami walked in through the doors and he jumped like he had been caught with his hand in the till. Ami stopped and frowned as she saw how close the woman had moved toward Sean. She copied the girls body language and placed her hands on her hips as well but this was not flirtatious. It was menacing. She walked over and said "Evening lover" and slid her arm around his waist.

"Hi Ami," he felt very uncomfortable and decided to extract them from the situation. "Maddy, can you go and find a guy called Geordie. He will give you the tour. Come on babe, let's grab a seat over here."

"See you... ...babe," said Maddy and headed for a group of people standing near the bar.

Sean held Ami's waist and started to move her toward a table. She immediately winced and pulled away. Sean initially thought she was pissed off with him but then realised she was in pain. Her hand was held against her ribs, protecting them from him touching her. As he looked closer he could see how heavy her makeup was. Under the light it was difficult to notice but he could see a black shadow covering her cheek. His rage built in a second. "Who the fuck has hit you? Whoever it is they are dead! It was that bloke I passed at your house wasn't it? I knew there was something wrong with him."

"Yes it was."

"Who is he and why did he lay his hands on you?"

"He's my husband."

Sean stepped back as if he had been punched in the face."

"Your husband? but you said you were divorced."

"Separated. For a long time but not divorced yet. He keeps trying to get me back."

"So why was he at your house and why did he hit you?"

"The day I met you he turned up at my place. He said he had been thrown out of his flat and needed a place to stay for a couple of days. Olivia begged me to help him so I said ok. Nothing happened initially but he started pestering me to give him another chance. When he saw you he asked who you were and I told him you were my boyfriend. He went mad and beat me. As soon as it was over he was filled with remorse but I said he had to go. Tomorrow he's out of my life forever. I know it is messy and not what you expected but I'm yours if you want me Sean. If not I will completely understand. Either way he's gone. I don't want Olivia near him."

"So, I'm your boyfriend am I? You know it's

traditional to ask first," he cracked a huge grin.

Ami winced as she got down on one knee. "Sean O'Shea, you arrogant bastard, will you be my boyfriend?"

He helped her up. "Ami, if he tries to touch you again, I will kill him."

"I know, I told him. It won't happen again and he is out of my life. He is babysitting tonight if you fancy a drink with me later." She kissed him hard on the lips, spun on her heels and walked out of the club.

"So is that your misses?," said Maddy sliding up behind him.

Sean didn't turn around. Instead he watched Ami as she strutted into the shadows at the main door. "Not yet, she's my girlfriend. Listen, I need to get some clean clothes for tonight. Tell Geordie not to disturb Bill, he's with his brief." Without looking in Maddy's direction he turned and walked to the back entrance to pick up his car.

EIGHT

"You make me sick," screamed Audrey. "You think I want anything to do with you. Why don't you die you bastard? You make out you're bloody Mister Perfect to outsiders, don't you think I don't know what you've been up to all these years with my girl? My daughter! You treat her like a whore, you filthy scum! You've wrecked Theresa's life and I wish you were dead!"

Sean had hardly opened the front door an inch before he heard his mum shouting at Ray.

His dads voice was beyond the limit of control. A loud crack filled the air as someone got slapped. "I fuck her 'cause you don't ever want me!"

"You sick bastard! How can you talk like that about your own child?"

That was enough, Sean's body filled with adrenalin and the red mist dropped in front of his eyes. He raised his shoulders, muscles tensed for murder and strode towards the kitchen door. As he passed the staircase a loud thud stopped him in his tracks. Above him a body had hit the floor. Theresa! Instantly his focus changed and he ran up the stairs three at a time. Outside the locked bathroom door he paused for a second before crashing through it like it was made of balsa wood. On the floor, his sister lay pale, lifeless, and surrounded by empty baggies. Sean fell to the floor and started CPR. Seconds later the door filled with his mum and dad. Audrey screamed but was drowned out by Sean.

"Call an ambulance, now!"

Audrey ran downstairs to get her phone as Ray stepped forward. Sean didn't stop working on his sister but looked back at his dad. "If she doesn't make it you won't need an ambulance. Just the fucking undertaker you sick bastard."

Ray backed away and walked downstairs to the front door. From a distance each step made him look like a zombi and, as he pulled on the door handle, he walked into the street and shrank into the distance.

In Sean's head it seemed like hours before the paramedics arrived, closely followed by an ambulance surrounded by a halo of two's and blues. In reality it was only twelve minutes.

As they entered the room he was gently moved to one side and they started to assess her condition.

"She's breathing again. You did a good job, now let us stabilise her." A needle was slid into her and what looked like a bucket of clear liquid entered her body. Sean stepped back feeling useless as his sister struggled for life.

A stretcher had made its way to the top of the stairs and Theresa was strapped onto it. She was breathing in spasms and he could only guess her heart was dancing inside her chest in the same way. "That's how white men dance man," said a voice out of his past. "No rhythm." Back in the day, when he worked the doors on high profile clubs, he had teamed up with a giant afro Caribbean guy called Ajay. Ajay always took the piss out of the sweaty white punters who desperately rubbed themselves against the girls on the dance floor. "That's not what women want," he said. "They want a man with rhythm because they know he will be good in bed. White men have no rhythm Sean, no good in the sack man." He had a huge grin on his face. Sean never rose to the bait but he was glad he had enough rhythm to get his sisters heart started again.

As Theresa was carried down the narrow staircase, he made a detour to his room. In the bedside drawer he found what he had wanted. Below a book and inside a brown leather sheath stamped with the letters "USMC" was a steel blade. It had five more letters driven into the metal. "KA-BAR" was visible on the Ricasso just below the finger guard. He pushed it back in place and slid it into the back of his belt. Ray was going to pay for this one way or another. He walked down the stairs and climbed into his car, ready to follow the ambulance as it left.

The hospital had been the worst experience of his life but the only place he had ever said "Thank God," and meant it. After two hours, the door at the end of the corridor swung open and a young doctor started the long walk towards Audrey and him. "She's out of the woods" he said. Sean thought it was an apt expression. It looked like Theresa had been lost in the woods for years. He just hadn't seen it. If it cost him everything, he vowed he would keep her in the light from now on. His mum too. How had no one told him what Ray was doing to them? He had always been a shit but even this was beyond anything Sean had imagined. His guts were twisted like barbed wire.

Later, the big Irishman sat outside the club with the Range Rovers engine idling. He had been staring at the instrument cluster and imagining the two main dials were eyes staring back at him. Theresa's eyes and they said "why did you leave me, why did you let this happen to me?" He had spent years living half a life with his wife, thinking he had it bad, but his sister had less than nothing. Her teenage years had been stolen from her. As he stepped out of the car, his temper was well into the redline. Now he was inside the club it blew off the scale.

Maddy was at the bar surrounded by Dan and the guy he had seen dealing outside. In front of them were three lines of half snorted coke. Sean stormed over.

"What the fuck are you playing at? He pointed at Maddy. "If Bill sees that, you're fucking out. Stay away from that prick, he's a loser. She looked down at the counter and said "Sorry," as she started to load the bar.

"And who are you? Fucking really?" He stepped towards Karl. Why are you always here and why are you hanging around my daughter? You pushing for Dan?"

Karl leaned back against the wall. "Dan, please tell him who the fuck he's speaking to. This is getting a bit boring now."

"Well, if ya didn't figure it yet," said Dan. "Karl's shagging Tasha. So, if you really want your daughter to actually like you one day, then be nice to him."

Sean cut him off. "Is that supposed to impress me? You think I give a rats arse? Get that shit off my bar and fuck off, now!"

He walked towards them aggressively. Karl and Dan backed away and walked out of the club laughing. "Fine, but it's not even mine. You always think the worst of me, just like your lovely uncle Bill. You are both Dickheads!"

Maddy stepped alongside him "I'm sorry Sean. It won't happen again."

"Maddy… …I don't care what you take, but not in this club. If I see it again you'll be sacked instantly. It's up to you." He stared sternly at Maddy before turning towards Bill's office and walking inside.

As he swung the door closed it stopped before it clicked into place. Tasha pushed it open and then slammed it behind her.

"What's your problem Sean?" she said.

"Don't call me Sean. I'm your father. Show some respect."

"Thats rich, Daddy!" She opened the door wide and Karl stepped through. Before it closed she began kissing him."

"Look if you want to ruin your life on that loser then go ahead, but did you know he and Dan were sniffing coke on my bar? That's why I chucked him out. That's the only reason."

He turned to Karl before she had a chance to answer. "If you ever get her on that gear you're a dead man and that is not an analogy. It's a fact you little scumbag."

"Dad'. I'll do what I like, when I like! You never cared before so you have no rights now."

He swung back towards her. "I never knew…" but she was gone, dragging Karl behind her. As her boyfriend closed the door he flashed a sickening grin at Sean.

"Time to start fixing things around here. I'm sick of firefighting. I need to get ahead of all of this shit," he said out loud.

"You starting to talk to yourself babe?" said Ami as she walked in.

He smiled at her. She looked amazing dressed in a tiny A line skirt, heels and a black top.

"You're not ready? I thought you were going to pick some clothes up. Did I dress up for no reason?"

"Yeah, it all went wrong. Ami, give me twenty minutes. Wait here. I'll get changed and get back. Have a drink at the bar. I need to tick something off my ToDo list and then we can enjoy the evening"

He kissed her and walked out.

At Ami's house Sean knocked on the door. It opened and the man he had passed on her path the other day stood in the doorway. "Yes?" he said.

"Where's Olivia?"

"She's upstairs watching YouTube. What's it got to do with you?"

Sean grabbed him by the throat and slammed him into the wall. "If you ever touch Ami again I'll fucking kill ya, you get me?" Sean's face was an inch from Ami's husband's.

"Sorry. It was an accident. Yes, sorry!"

Sean punched him in the guts and walked to the gate. He then looked back to the man, doubled over on the floor. As he began to leave he stopped. In the blink of an eye Sean spun around and kicked him in the head. "Oops, that was a nasty accident wasn't it. Sometimes sorry just won't cut it."

Ami sat in the same booth she shared with her friends the first night. Maddy had brought her a drink and the two had exchanged dirty looks. Finally Sean returned and sat down opposite her. "I thought you were only going to be a few moments. What happened?"

"I got waylaid. Look, do you mind a change of plans? I've had such a shit day. Can we stay in at my place? I'll cook and we can chill out."

"Sounds perfect."

"Let's go, before anything else gets screwed up." He put his arm around her waist and she leaned into him as they walked to his car.

Twenty minutes later he was pouring her a glass of

wine. She picked it up, kissed him gently on the lips and then walked into the bedroom. "Bring a drink lover, you're going to need it." She turned away and slipped out of her shoes as she left.

Sean poured a giant glass of wine, dropped his jacket on the chair and followed in her footsteps.

The next morning he woke as Ami was climbing back into her clothes.

"You need a lift?"

"No thanks. My place is not very far and I need to change before work."

"Will I see you later?"

"Maybe but I have to look after Olivia. I'll call and let you know. By the way, last night was wonderful."

They shared a moment and then she was gone.

He lay back and stared at the ceiling. The pillow smelled of her perfume. "This whole thing is getting intense," he said and then slid out of bed to have a shower.

Dan had had better days. After telling Sean that Karl was screwing his daughter, he drove away from the club with the dealer in his car. "Are you feeding her a steady supply of Coke?"

"Yes I'm doing exactly what you told me. She's getting dependant. It won't be long before I tell her the supply has dried up and then I can get her into smack. Then she is fucked. It will be a few weeks before she is turning tricks to pay for it. Why do you hate her that much?"

"I couldn't give a fuck about her. I want Sean to know his little girl spends her time making money on her back. He won't look so great then will he, his whore daughter fucking anyone to get enough money to pay for her drugs."

"You are an evil bastard Dan."

"You getting a conscience Karl?"

"No but I need more money to finance her free Blow. She's going through it like sweets.

"Open the glove box. Take the envelope. Its got ten grand in there. That will pay for her and leave you with a nice payday as well."

Karls face lit up. "Cheers Dan. I'll make certain she's completely fucked up in a month."

"Good. In the meantime, keep away from Sean. If he finds out what's happening he'll fucking kill you."

"Don't worry, I work best behind the scenes. He won't see anything until it's too late."

Dan pulled to the curb and dropped Karl outside Tasha's. "Get it done quickly. There'll be a nice bonus the first time she turns a trick."

Karl nodded and walked to the door searching for a key in his pockets. "You home Tasha? Thought we could get a takeaway tonight," he called as the door clicked closed behind him.

Dan drove back to his house and parked in the drive. As he stepped up to the house three dark shapes separated from the shadows and one of them swung a baseball bat as hard as possible. It caught Dan on the back, knocked him forward smashing his head into the brickwork.

He couldn't work out how long he had been out but he knew he was in deep shit when he slowly realised he was cable tied to a chair in his kitchen.

"What the fuck do you want?" he said.

"Nothing. Absolutely nothing. This is a simple message for your family. The Dolans are back and you need to adapt to the new reality you are living in," said

Tony Dolan, the big man in front of him. The other two kept looking out of the window keeping an eye on the street. "Bill isn't going to be around for ever. It's time you decided how you want to run the business when he's gone. We would much prefer you were in charge than that crazy fucking cousin of yours."

"Fuck you!" Dan said, but the idea had already started to make him think. "You want me to be a good boy while your lot takes over?"

"Exactly that. You catch on quick. In return we will let you keep the club and run a modest operation as long as we get a cut."

"Pay you? Are you kidding. We rule here."

"You ruled here. Past tense. Let me help you understand." He drove a ham sized fist into Dan's eye quickly followed by three more well placed punches that left him with a broken nose, a chipped tooth and blood covering half his face. "Getting the picture?" Tony said. Just to make certain he was maintaining Dans attention he drove five more massive blows to the mans ribs cracking at least one in the process.

"Ok, I fucking get it. So what are you going to do about Sean?" said Dan.

"Leave him to us. Just make certain you remember today. I don't want to have to repeat this conversation," he leant into Dan's broken face. "Do I?"

"Ok, ok, I got the message."

As Tony left he pushed Dan's chair. It tipped back and slammed his head onto the floor. For the second time that night Dan lost consciousness. When he woke up in the early hours he had two thoughts crystal clear in his head. First, he would be happy to let Tony have a crack at taking Sean out, it would save him the trouble. Second, the Dolans had to be sorted one way or another when things had settled down.

It was just before nine in the morning when Mickey turned up and found Dan still tied to the chair. By that time Dan had pissed himself and needed to shower before he could report to Bill at the club.

Now he was sitting in a chair on the opposite side of his dad's desk with Ray perching on the edge in front of him. "What did they want?" said Ray. "and why did they let you go so easily?"

"Fucking easily?" said Dan. "You call this easy?" he shouted pulling the bag of ice away from his purple cheek bone. "They beat the fuck out of me!"

"But you are still alive. Why?"

"Ray's right Dan. They had you and let you go. After what we did, you should be floating down the Thames right now."

Dan bristled. No one gave a fuck about how much he was hurt. "I don't have a fucking clue Ray. Maybe they were dazzled by my good looks. All I know is they said this was a message to us. They are pissed about the mess Sean caused. They said they are in the driving seat around here now and Sean is going to get us killed if he isn't controlled."

At that moment Dan's cousin walked through the door. "What the fuck happened to you?" Sean asked Dan. "You trip over your high heels walking down the stairs to the ladies?"

Dan started to climb to his feet but the broken rib stopped him in his tracks. He sat back down slowly. "No, your stupid idea of a shoot up with the Dolan's heavies had consequences and, as always, they affect other people not you. Tony was pissed off with your wild west attitude."

Sean looked at Bill. "We need to finish this."

Bill nodded. "Take Dan, Ray and Mickey. Make certain there is no comeback after this one."

"I don't need Dan and Mickey. Best if we keep the main family as far away from this as possible. I can handle this with Ray."

His dad looked up quickly. "Just the two of us?"

"We'll use an outside pair of hands to help. Someone that can't be traced to us. He's an old mate and very reliable."

Bill turned around to the safe and pulled out three silenced pistols, matching boxes of ammo plus matching clips to hold them. "Fix it Sean, once and for all."

"No problem," he said and followed Ray out of the door.

Dan looked at Bill and said "Hopefully he won't fuck it up this time."

"Sean is helping all of us. Give him some credit."

Dan got up and walked out the back door. When he got to the alley he saw their car turn into the main street. "I'll give him exactly what he deserves." He smiled as he pulled out is phone and began typing a persons name. After the first three letters were entered it automatically suggested a contact. Dan clicked on the name and punched in a message. When he hit send the screen returned to the contact. Dan clicked the phone off and Tony Dolan's name disappeared.

NINE

"Serj," Sean was on the phone as Ray drove through the quiet backstreets. "I need you to help out with a bit of trouble. The Dolans. I've got one for you. Meet at the road outside their yard in fifteen minutes. Cheers." He pressed the screen and the call ended. "He'll meet us there."

"You sure we can trust him?" asked Ray "I don't like working with people I don't know."

"I know him. I'd trust him with my life. In fact, I've had to several times before. He's a safe pair of hands when it comes to this stuff."

As they pulled up to the corner outside the Dolan's yard he could see Serj in the distance. "Wait here a minute."

Sean crossed the street and stood with his back to Ray's car. Thanks for coming."

"No problem. You know I'm always there for you man."

"Likewise. Now here's the plan. I will do whoever is in the office. It's the big portacabin over there. After that I'll deal with the guy in the driver's seat of the car behind me."

Serj looked over Sean's shoulder. "Ok. Who's the bloke you are with then? An informant?"

"No, he's my dad."

"Fuck Sean! Are you certain?"

"Yes I'm certain and don't ask why."

"When have you known me to ask. It's enough you want it done. I'll assume it's important."

"Yes it is."

He walked back to the Range Rover. "Let's go. All you have to do is keep an eye on the door behind us and make certain no one is going to shoot us in the back."

"Ok," said Ray. He followed his son back to Serj and the three of them walked steadily to the cabins front door.

The big Irishman kicked it off its hinges and they raised their guns in unison. Inside, Tony was sitting at a table with five other men. As the door exploded, they all jumped to their feet and started to grab for gun holsters in their jackets.

"No, no, no! Keep the hands down lads." Inside the room every man froze with fingers wrapped around pistols still stuck in their holsters. Sean and Serj pointed guns randomly at the group while Ray watched the yard from the doorway. "Good! Now keep dead still or you *will* be dead. Hello Tony. Seems we have a problem doesn't it?"

"No problem Sean. Your family is finished after today. We'll be taking over and there's fuck all you can do about it. The door business is already ours and so are your smuggling connections. Everybody has chosen sides and you are shit out of luck so take your poxy friends and wait at the club until I send you orders." He pulled out a massive cigar. The label said "Cohiba with smaller letters underneath that told you it had started life in Havana, Cuba. As Tony climbed to his feet bullets began flying past his head and he instantly curled into a ball under his seat. Sean and Serj nailed everyone around him with one round to the chest and another to the head. Within seconds Tony was on his own facing the two men whose gun barrels still had small swirls of smoke rising from the suppressers. As the last of the bodies finally hit the floor, everything became silent. Outside footsteps ran towards the hut. A man turned into the doorway and Ray fired three bullets into his chest. The man spun sideways and collapsed to the floor. There was a slight thud as someone bumped along the outside of the wall. A classic mistake for anyone who has spent little time around guns. Timber walls are no match for large calibre shells at this range. Serj and Sean opened fire at the same time and five holes appeared in the wall allowing light to stream through them. By the time the man's body had fallen onto the gravel they had both ejected their clips and had full magazines back in place.

Ray just stared at them. "Fuck me, it's the Rambo twins. You two are mental."

Serj and Sean looked at each other and then at Ray. They lifted their guns at the same time and pointed them directly at his head.

"What the fuck are you doing?"

"Drop the gun Ray. Now!" His dad let the pistol drop to the floor. "Keep your gun on him Serj." Sean walked up to Tony and slid his hand inside the man's jacket. As he pulled his hand back it held a Smith and Western .44 revolver. "Big gun for a little man," said Sean. He took the cigar away from Tony as well. "Business must be good. This is a fifty quid note you were about to light up." He ignored Tony and turned back to Ray.

"Sean what are you up to?" Ray had a quiver in his voice.

"Do you think I wouldn't have found out eventually? How long have you kept your dirty secret?"

Ray looked horrified. "What do you mean? Why the fuck are you pointing a gun at me?"

Seans anger boiled over and he cocked Tony's revolver and lifted it to Rays face.

"What did you expect?" said Ray. "She was having his baby and I loved her. We were young. Wouldn't you have done the same?"

"What the fuck are you talking about Ray? Whose baby?"

Ray hadn't heard a word Sean said, he was starting to babble. "I loved her first! The jammy bastard knew that. He stole her from me. I'm more of a dad than that piece of filth would've been to ya. Blood or no. He belongs in the grave I put him in, Sean. You must know that?"

Serj had lost track of what was either of them were talking about. "For fuck sake! What's going on here?" He said.

Sean ignored Serj and lowered the gun slightly but still kept it pointing at his dad. "Hang on, you saying what I think you're saying? Are you talking about me?"

"Well, that's what you are on about, isn't it?

"You killed my dad!? You're not my real dad at all?"

"Wait a minute, have I got this wrong?

"That's why you never liked me. For years I've never understood you. What's fucking wrong with you? So, what's the reason you've been screwing your daughter?" Ray looked like he had been slapped in the face. Sean lifted the gun again.

"This is about Theresa?" Ray stared at the end of the gun. "She's a slut, Sean. Probably not even my blood either. She's been putting it about for a bit of blow. Gagging for it. Let's not fall out over some..."

The Smith and Western weighed just over three and a half pounds but it took less than half that to pull the trigger. A .44 magnum bullet left the end of the barrel and removed most of Rays head. Compared to the silenced pistols this thing was a cannon. Sean's ears were ringing and he barely heard Tony shouting behind him. "The O'Shea's are all fucking mental."

Sean finally tuned back in, turned around and used his 9mm to fill Tony's chest with half a dozen bullets before putting one between his eyes. Tony's lifeless corpse lay on the floor with one hand held out towards his killer as if to hold hands. Sean walked over, wiped down the revolver and pushed it into the dead mans fingers. Once the scene was staged he was about to walk out with Serj when something buzzed on the table. A little voice in Sean's head told him to turn around. Under a pile of twenty pound notes was a phone. He touched the screen and a picture of Tony with some brassy tart in a skin tight minidress draped on his arm lit up. The signal strength was virtually non existent and the tiny metre in the top right hand corner periodically lit up the first bar before it disappeared. Half way down the screen was a message in preview mode. At the top there was a single name. Below it were the words "Sean is on his way and he's armed." He looked back to the name. "Dan," it said. Serj was behind him. "What the fuck? Why would your cousin warn him? We got lucky, it must have been stuck because the reception is bad here. Otherwise we would have had a big party of armed twats waiting for us."

Sean put the phone in his pocket and walked back to the car with Serj just behind him.

At the Range Rover the Irishman took Serj's gun and climbed in. "I'll get rid of these."

His friend leaned on the door and started laughing. "Sean my man, you are the craziest fucker I have ever met."

"Not a word about this Serj. It never happened."

"What never happened ?" said Serj still laughing."

"Exactly. Now, do me a favour, find out everything about Dan, who is he involved with and what he has up his sleeve. Tony would never have let him go. Something doesn't make sense."

"Of course, my friend. Speak soon." Serj walked back to his car and drove off.

Sean picked up his mobile phone and called Bill.

"I'm sorry, it's all gone pear shaped. Dad's been killed. I'm the only one left. The rest are dead. I'll come to the club."

"No Sean. Go home and clean up, change your clothes and then come back to the club. Don't tell your mum yet. I'll do it. Sean?"

"Yes Bill."

"Are you OK?"

"Yeah, I'm ok." He hung up the phone and sat back in his seat. After a few seconds he started the engine and slid the car into gear. Before he drove away he said "No more worries for you sis, you're safe now." He spun the wheel, buried the accelerator and drove west, back to his apartment.

Bill had spent the rest of the morning making calls. The first one was to Slippery. He told him to be on standby, just in case.

Next he spoke to a couple of bent coppers who he knew would end up part of the investigation team. They were told to keep him updated and run defence where possible.

Finally he spoke to an undertaker. They had helped the family many times over the years and now it was time for them to start work preparing his brothers funeral. After the call he sat staring at the phone. He couldn't work out why he didn't feel more upset. Yeah, Ray had always been a bit of a tosser but now Bill felt pleased he was gone. Then he realised he was happy. Not that Ray was dead but that Sean was alive. As he put his feelings together, his nephew walked into his office. He was dressed in a different pair of jeans with a leather jacket over the top. The black bomber he had worn when he left with Ray was gone. No doubt burnt by now.

As Sean closed the door Bill strode over and put his arm around the younger man.

"Come and grab a seat and tell me what happened."

"It all happened quickly Bill. Like they knew we were coming."

"I said take the others, didn't I?"

"Yes but that wasn't the problem. We could easily have taken them out but they were already tooled up and on alert."

"Does mum know yet?"

"Not unless you told her. We've just got to wait, just as if nothing happened. At least until the old bill get here.

Sean nodded but then looked Bill in the eye. "Tell me Bill. Ray, I mean, dad said something weird before he died.

"Like what?"

"He said he wasn't my dad. That he had killed my real dad in some kind of love battle.

Bill walked to his chair and sat down. "It's all bollocks. He was your dad and that's that." He broke eye contact again.

"You knew, didn't ya Bill?"

"I know nothing. Now, stop this."

"For fuck sake, Bill! Who was my real dad?" Sean

slammed his hand down on the desk. "Who was he and why weren't I told?"

"Leave it Sean."

"No, I have a right to know." Bill looked at Sean sternly and then decided to say nothing else. Sean got up, walked through the club and into the street.

Ami had been doing housework so was pleased when she got the call from Sean asking her out to lunch. As she hung up the phone her ex husband walked into the room sporting a blue bruise where he had been pinned against the wall the day before. "It was him wasn't it?"

"Yes and he's taking me for lunch. I want you gone when I get back."

"I thought I could stay one more night," he said.

"That ship has sailed. Take your stuff and leave us alone." Ami didn't wait for a reply, she just grabbed her coat and walked to the cafe on the green where she had first talked with Sean. He was already sitting outside at the same table they had before.

As she approached, his face lit up and he welcomed her with a huge hug.

"Are you ok?" she said.

"Not so much," he looked concerned "let me tell you the story so far."

Twenty minutes later Ami's jaw was nearly resting on the table. Sean had started by telling her Ray was dead. He omitted the part where he had used Tony's revolver to lobotomise him. He also didn't say anything about what Ray had been up to with his sister. It still sickened him just thinking about it. Next he explained Ray's last words had been a confession of sorts about killing Sean's real father, whoever that was.

When she finally managed to close her mouth she walked around the table, sat in his lap and held him as tight as she could. For the first time that day, Sean felt like things would be ok.

"Listen, are you due any holiday? Fancy getting away?" he asked.

"What you mean just us or the kids as well?"

"Just us would be good but whatever. Would your ex look after Olivia?"

"He won't be around anymore but she will be able to stay at her friends for a few days."

"Then let me book something for us."

"Ok, but after the funeral, obviously?"

Sean ignored her and wrapped his giant arms around Ami like he was protecting her from a world filled with evil.

The next day she parked her car at the back of the club. Ami had used her free morning to pop into a few travel agents and now had an armful of brochures for the two of them to look through. At the door she could hear voices directly behind it. She recognised that one was Dan's. He was talking quietly but the other man sounded pissed off.

"My fucking brother is dead! He offered you a deal and the next minute one of your lot guns him down and half a dozen of our men. We both know who the mad fucker is that did it. If you ever want to run your business you need to help us put this right."

Dan's voice stayed calm in comparison. "I wasn't there. I sent Tony a warning but it didn't make any difference. Now you need to fuck off and leave this to me for now if you ever want this to work."

The door opened in front of Ami and she jumped

back.

"Whose this nosey little tart?" said a tall man with two days of stubble covering his face.

"Ignore her, she's just a local slag that hangs around the club," smirked Dan.

Ami pulled herself together and pushed past the men.

The tall man left and Dan followed Ami into the hallway. "He's not here."

"What?"

"Sean's not here. He's off somewhere. I think he took our new barmaid back to his flat to give her some one-to-one coaching."

"It won't work Dan. I know Sean isn't like that."

"You have no idea who Sean is or what he's like."

For a second she hesitated and then decided to leave especially if her man wasn't here anyway. As she tried to go back past Dan he grabbed her hair and pushed her against the wall. His free hand began to pull up her skirt. "You cheap tart. I'm sick of you pretending you are whiter than white. I know he fucked you out back. Now I'm going to give it to you like Sean can't." She kicked at him, desperately trying to push him off "You like it rough do ya? So, let's have some rough for the little rough bitch?"

"Get off me, you bastard!" Years of abuse had built up inside her and she was determined she wasn't going to let herself get put in that situation again. With all her strength she pushed back and managed to throw him off for a second. Turning towards him, she slapped his face and, while the clap was echoing in the hallway, she kicked him in the nuts as hard as she could.

Dan opened his mouth to scream in pain but

nothing came out. Instead he fell to the floor as if he had been thrown out of a window.

Ami burst through the exit crying and laughing at the same time. Without hesitating, she jumped into the car and drove as fast as she dared to Sean's apartment building.

By the time she arrived her mascara had run down her cheeks and it was stinging her eyes. It made it difficult to ring the correct number on the door pad. After trying several times and getting nowhere she was about to give up when she heard a familiar voice "Can I help you miss?" As she turned around Sean's big smile disappeared when he saw she had been crying.

"What happened?"

Relief overwhelmed her and she began sobbing again.

"Calm down Ami, tell me."

"He...He grabbed me...And touched me!"

"I'll fucking kill him! I told him I would... Is he at your house?"

"No, no, no…Not him...It wasn't my ex, it was Dan!"

"DAN? Fucking hell! Did he, you know, rape you?"

"No...he tried to...but I managed to get away."

Sean opened the door and led her to the elevator. Within seconds they were inside his apartment and she was curled up safe on the sofa.

"Babe, stay here. I won't be long. Shall I call a friend over to look after you?"

"No I'll be OK, just hurry back."

He forced a weak smile on his face to be as consoling as possible. It didn't work. All Ami saw was a twisted mask of a man that had murder on his mind. She thought she should feel sorry for Dan but in her head a voice shouted out "Fuck him!"

From the front door of the club it was exactly one hundred and twenty eight feet to Bill's desk in the office. Sean's stride ate the ground at over two metres a second so twenty one seconds after he entered the building a massive punch lifted Dan into the air and knocked him backwards across Bill's desk. As he slowly climbed to his feet he said "Is that the best you have got?" But there was no conviction in his voice that said he wanted to find out. The little bravado he had mustered up disappeared and Sean pressed the loud end of a revolver into Dans temple. His head was sandwiched against the wall.

"He's finally lost it, dad," screamed Dan.

Bill didn't move but shouted "Sean, calm down!"

"Tell them! Tell them what you fucking did you piece of shit!" Sean hissed into Dans ear.

"I've no idea what he's talking about."

The barrel of gun pressed harder into Dan's temple.

"You're making it very easy for me to pull this trigger. "Now, I'm going to give you one more chance to come clean."

"Well, it's like this; Ami wanted a real good fucking, so she came to see me. Begged me to sort her out because her boyfriend here couldn't satisfy the dirty little slag."

The butt of a gun isn't made to be soft to the touch. Its hard steel and resin, so when Sean's revolver hit Dan in the head it wasn't surprising he fell to his knees screaming. Just as he stopped Sean kicked him in the gut knocking all of the wind out of him.

"Sean stop," shouted Bill. "I get it... I get it." The

old man grabbed his nephew by the arm. "Put the gun down. Please!" He gently steered the big guy away when Dan started screaming hysterically.

"You ain't got the balls Sean, have ya? You're pathetic. You don't deserve the O'Shea name.

Without an expression on his face, Sean turned to Dan and shot him through the leg. He spun back to his uncle. "Sorry Bill but he had be taught. Now sort him out or the next time I put a bullet in him will be to put this sick rapist down."

"Dan rolled across the floor crying in pain as Sean walked out.

Bill turned to Mickey. "Get him up to the hospital and say you found him like that and that he had been robbed.

"Ok dad."

Bill looked down at his eldest son slowly bleeding onto the carpet. "What are you playing at Dan? This has got to stop! You behave like a fucking spoilt kid! Why can't you act more like..?" but decided not to finish the sentence.

Dan knew exactly who Bill meant and it tore at his wound even more.

TEN

Gary Dolan hated talking to Dan. When Ami had surprised them at the club he felt like someone had watched him stand in dog shit. Leaving felt like scraping it off.

He couldn't rely on the pathetic weasel to run their family's business let alone deal with Sean O'Shea. It would be like expecting a rabbit to make a good job of owning a pet Hyena. You knew it was going to turn out bad from the start.

Now he was standing in a stately home, in the middle of the night, holding a Picasso, ragged at the edges where he had cut it out of the frame. Normally this would be a booked-to-order theft but for Gary it was a means to an end.

He rolled it carefully, slid it into a cardboard tube and handed it to one of his gang. "Let's go, it's time to play Santa."

It was the next evening when Sean and Ami finally got to talk over what had happened at the club. His apartment was filled with dim pools of light and Ami was sitting in one of them stretched out on the sofa. The sound on the television was muted but she could read the ticker tape at the bottom of the newsreaders screen. "Rare Picasso stolen from property tycoons house," slowly scrolled from right to left.

"Someone got rich last night," she said as Sean walked over with a bottle of Champagne and two glasses.

"Not really, it will be virtually impossible to fence. Its ok if it was stolen to order but most of these robberies are speculative. Maybe in a few years they could sell it if they could find a bent specialist who knows how to get rid of it safely, but that expertise and risk comes at a massive price. After all that work, they would do well to make 20% of it's market value. If they don't get caught. Maybe split 4 ways that's about 100 grand a year each over two years. If one of them grassed up the others, the reward would pay them more. Too much risk, too many things could go wrong."

"You sound like you have some experience," she said with a smirk on her face.

"Who me?" The grin on his face said everything.

Ami played along. "What did you do Sean O'Shea?"

"I might have dabbled in the art world at one time. My dabbles might also have introduced me to one of Her Majesty's free hotels for a couple of years."

She was shocked for a second but then remembered some of the tall tales she had heard about him. They weren't so tall after all. "That must have been hard. Two years is a long time."

"The worst was being away from the family. That and the boredom. I was lucky. The day I arrived my cell had a welcome food parcel courtesy of the family. At that time they ran most of the nicks in the south of England. By the first afternoon, Dick "the cleaver" Woods, nice guy but a murderer by trade, had made me some curtains and fitted them to the window over my bunk."

"Now you are taking the Mickey."

"Straight up. I don't need to exaggerate my time in there. It was mad enough as it was. My life was cushy. As a bit of a legend and one of the O'Shea's, I got a privileged job in a side room to the kitchen. I actually put on weight while I was in. It was good eating for some. We got first choice of the food before anyone else and ran a black market in scarce commodities."

"What were scarce commodities in prison?"

"Penguin chocolate bars were like money. The nonces were turned upside down for theirs every week."

"Penguins? You are a gangster aren't you," she said sarcastically.

In a cheesy fake American accent he said "Hey listen, I roll with the big dogs honey." Ami laughed.

"So it cannot have always been easy jobs and chocolate bars."

Sean's face clouded for a minute. "I said I had it easy, not good. I told you, the separation was bad but the boredom killed people, literally. I'm not a big drug user but even I had puffed some Rocky, Lebanese or Black when it was available. Others sold their soul and everything else for harder shit. Whatever made the day pass more quickly. Other than that there were a lot of turf wars. While I was in, the Russians decided they wanted our piece of the action. They rushed our back room armed with a makeshift shiv. Stabbed a couple of our people badly."

"Were you hurt?"

"No. I came out of it well. After the initial madness I was left in the room with three of them. They expected me to run but they shit themselves when I kicked the door closed."

"But they were armed"

Sean smiled "Ami, I worked in a kitchen. A place filled with butcher knives. Only these fuck wits would try to start a fight with people surrounded by weapons."

"But did you get hurt?"

"Put it this way, I was the only one who walked out at the end."

For a second she imagined what might have happened but then shook it off. All she had seen Sean do is protect her. She liked that feeling. It was the first time in her life she wasn't scared by anything around her. She leaned back and tucked her feet under her body. "Are you going to pour that Champagne or should we just watch it slowly evaporate?"

"Of course my Princess, whatever you command." He handed her a glass and then slid down beside her. "I'm glad we met Ami. I think things are going to work out for us."

"Me too. To us lover." She clinked his glass and they looked each other in the eyes as they drank deep.

Sean put his glass on the coffee table. "Food?" he asked.

"Later," said Ami and pulled him onto her lips.

When they eventually broke the kiss he looked down at her. "Usually I expect to be bought dinner before I put out."

"Of course you do Sean. Consider this an IOU for later." She pushed him back, sat on his chest and stared into his eyes. "I love you. Is that payment enough?"

"Works for me," he said "and I love…" He didn't get to finish his sentence because her mouth had already closed over his.

Audrey had decided to spend some time at May's house. When Bill had turned up on the doorstep and asked for a cup of tea, she had known Ray or Sean were dead. When he said it was her husband she burst into tears. Bill had tried to calm her down saying it was going to be a huge shock for anyone losing their husband but he had read it wrong. Her tears were relief. Relief her son was alive and grateful Ray was dead. "Sometimes people do get what they deserve," she thought but didn't say it to Bill.

When he suggested she stay with mad Aunt May, it sounded like a holiday compared to what she had lived with for the past few years. Within an hour she had packed and Bill had kindly dropped her at their relatives. That is why, when Gary Dolan and two of his men turned up at ten that night the house was silent and dark.

"Perfect," he thought. "This makes it easy. Soon Sean would be a out of his hair."

The man next to him had been working on the lock for about a minute and it slowly clicked open. "All yours boss," he said with a degree of satisfaction in a job well done.

Gary pushed through the door and turned up the stairs. At the top of the landing he shone the light from his phone at the ceiling. Three feet in front of him was a hatch into the loft. He reached up, pushed hard and watched as a ladder dropped to the ground.

Behind him he could see his men standing guard just outside the front door. He turned and made his way into the attic. Still using the phone, he crouched and made his way to the back of the roof. From inside his jacket, a long tube slid into his hand. He was careful to place it in a position it would be impossible to miss if the space was searched. Making his way back to the steps, he climbed back down, slid the ladder back into place and closed the hatch.

"Merry Christmas Sean, you prick," he said as he made it to the bottom of the stairs and stepped into the night air.

"And a happy new year." said a voice behind him.

Gary spun around, just as a baseball bat crashed into his teeth leaving most of them shattered. He fell back onto the path between his two men.

To the left, one of them lay unconscious on the ground with his knee bent at an impossible angle. To the right, the other man was bleeding from a shattered nose and broken cheek bone.

"What the fuck?" Gary tried to say through what was left of his mouth. It sounded more like "Wath te fuff."

Serj stepped into the light, lifted the bat again and put Dolan's lights out with a solid blow to his temple.

"Night night, you stupid bastard," he said, grabbing the collar of the big mans jacket. He dragged the body to the back of his car and started stuffing it inside.

By the time Serj left, Gary was cable tied around his wrists and ankles with a piece of gaffer tape holding what was left of his mouth closed.

Two days earlier, Serj had been sitting drinking coffee at a little cafe behind 8ish. He was watching Dan's car and starting to regret telling Sean he would help find out what his mental cousin was up to. In 48 hours he had watched Dan go from home to the club and from the club to home twice. The rest of the time he was sat on his arse doing nothing. The only two interesting things of note were Dan meeting up with some scrawny bloke that Serj had seen pushing drugs on the street around the corner. The second thing that really spiked his interest was when Ami had turned up at the door to the rear door of the club. She had surprised Dan and a big bloke just as the latter was leaving.

As Dan followed Ami back inside the club, Serj decided to chance his arm by following the other man.

He pulled on a black crash helmet and climbed on the bike. As the big mans car pulled out at the end of the street Serj hit the starter and carefully tailed the man until he arrived at a yard a few miles away.

As the car emptied he pulled up at the corner and watched. A couple of boys were kicking a ball at a wall on the other side of the street. "Hey! You two local?" The boys were about twelve going on eighteen.

"What the fuck's it got to do with you?" said the taller of the two.

"I'll tell you what it's got to do with me. If I could find someone local I'd offer them twenty quid if they could tell me who that big guy is talking to those other men."

"Each?"

"What?"

"Twenty each."

"Fuck me boys, at least Dick Turpin had the decency to wear a mask when he was robbing people."

"We don't know any Dick Turpin but we know who he is and it will cost you twenty each."

Serj pulled some notes out of his pocket. "Come on, impress me with your knowledge," he said waving the money in front of their faces.

"You're not from round here are you. Everyone knows who that is. That's Gary Dolan." The boy snatched the cash just in case the man on the motorbike changed his mind.

Serj looked into the distance "Gary fucking Dolan. Dan you sneaky little shit." He turned back to the boys. "Cheers lads. How would you like to make double that tomorrow?"

The two boys looked at each other grinning and nodding.

"Do you have phones?"

Both of the boys produced iPhones and waved them in the air.

"When he arrives and leaves each day text this number." Serj reeled off his mobile. "If you do a good job there'll be more the day after." He handed the extra cash over and the boys moved closer to the gates to get a better view.

A day later, Dan got shot and ended up in hospital. Serj now decided it would be a better use of his time to follow Dolan. As soon as he got the text he had arrived Serj packed a bag into his car with a few essentials. Drinks, food, a Glock and a shiny aluminium baseball bat. "Better to be prepared." He drove to Dolan's yard and watched from a safe distance. Just after lunch he took a stroll towards the end of the road. The boys were sitting playing on their phones while watching the entrance.

"See that phone box over there," he said. "When I walk past I'll put another fifty quid in there for you. Keep up the good work."

"Are you the cops?" asked one of the boys.

"No, he left his kids and wife without any money and now I'm following him to try to help get them something to live on." Serj gambled that at least one of them was from a broken home. From the looks on their faces he guessed they both were. This way they would be less likely to sell him out to Gary for more money.

He walked back to the car, dropped off the cash and watched one of the boys follow him and pick it off the top of the phone.

At about 9pm Gary climbed into his 4x4 with two other men. All of them were wearing black and Serj guessed something was about to happen.

What he didn't expect was to be pulling up outside Sean's parents house about 45 minutes later.

He watched as the three of them huddled around the entrance. After a moment, the door opened and Gary walked in. The other two waited outside.

Serj leant into the backseat. A gun was out of the question at Sean's mums home. He slid the bat out of the bag, opened the car door and made his way around the side of the neighbours house.

After jumping the side fence he was able to work his way back towards the front. As he stepped out of the dark the bat was already in mid swing and smashed the knee of the first man and a second blow to his head meant he was unconscious before he hit the ground. The second man opened his mouth to shout a warning but Serj stabbed the end of the bat straight into his nose. As he reeled backwards, he met with the bat again but this time it was the mans cheek and his world turned black.

Serj walked into the house and quietly walked into the kitchen. Just as he arrived, footsteps crossed the landing above him. They started down the stairs and Serj matched their speed so Gary got to the door two feet in front of the baseball bat.

"Merry Christmas Sean, you prick," said Gary. Behind him the bat was already swinging towards him.

"And a happy new year." said Serj with a big smile on his face.

Tasha had been steadily snorting a larger mountain

of coke everyday for a week. Karl left her with an endless supply and never asked for any money. He really cared for her. Not like her shit of a dad. Sean hadn't even sent her a birthday card once in all these years. The anger had been building all day and now she was at her mums it was not about to stop.

"What the fuck did you see in him mum. He's a selfish bastard."

"Look Tasha, he's not that bad. I remember he was nice to me."

"Nice mum? He is so nice he knocked you up, fucked off and hasn't ever visited his daughter once," she screamed at the top of her voice.

"Tasha…"

"No mum. I'm sick of you defending him. He needs to be told what he has done to our lives." She grabbed her car keys and stormed out of the door.

"Tasha, stop," shouted her mum but her daughter's car was already racing away down the street towards Soho and the club.

Donna grabbed her keys, ran to her car and started the engine. As she checked the mirror she caught sight of herself. "Donna, you silly cow, you've cocked this up good and proper."

She turned the wheel and headed off in her daughters tracks.

Sean had never raised his voice once to Bill. It was a relationship built out of respect and completely the opposite to the one he had with Ray. But right now he couldn't control himself. "That bastard has been nothing but pure evil Bill," he shouted. At last mum and Theresa can live a proper life now."

Bill walked up to Sean and grabbed his shoulders.

"What's that supposed to mean. Ray was never a saint I know, but he was still my brother."

"Don't play the innocent with me. This family has so many bloody secrets, most of which you're involved in," Sean calmed his voice. Bill, you need to be on the level with me now. Enough is enough."

Bill sat back on the desk. His shoulders dropped and he opened his mouth. "At last," thought Sean. "I've gotten through to him."

The door flew open and Tasha burst in fifty percent crying, fifty percent screaming and one hundred percent incoherent.

As she stood in the doorway shouting Sean said sarcastically "Great timing as always."

Tasha slowed down. "Oh, I'm very bloody sorry. I forgot the world revolves around Sean bloody O'Shea!"

Donna ran into the room just behind her daughter.

"Oh good, a family reunion," said Sean He knew the moment was gone with Bill. Now he had to deal with another shit-storm in his life.

Donna pushed past Tasha and stood in front of Sean. "We need to talk."

"It's a bit late for that! Why was I kept in the dark? I had a right to know. It's not like it didn't matter. Jesus, I have a kid I know nothing about Donna. Why the secret?"

Donna turned to face her daughter as the room fell silent. Tasha stared from one to the other trying to catch her breath. She felt like she had taken a punch to her chest. The blow wasn't helping clear her head but finally she managed "What? He didn't fucking know?"

"Donna stepped forward. "Tasha…" but it was too late. Tasha couldn't think. Air, she needed air. The room suddenly felt like a vacuum.

She ran. A second later Donna bolted after her.

Bill grabbed Sean's arm. "It's my fault, all my fault." He also felt like there was no air. As he tried to talk. His chest felt tight but he needed to speak. "I didn't tell you. They both thought you knew. I was supposed to tell you."

"What the fuck Bill?" Sean shook off the old man's grip and ran after the two women.

As he burst into the street it was silent. No running footsteps, no crying, no one but him, alone again.

ELEVEN

The Dog, as everyone knew it, was a Mecca for the local scum, druggies and general dregs of society. As pubs go, The Dog and Duck started life as an East End icon. At its height in the sixties it was frequented by both gangland royalty as well as royalty wanting to mix with the gang lords. Anything could be bought, sold or imbibed at the Dog, including things that didn't need to be poured into a glass.

As always, time catches up with every old lady and it hadn't missed The Dog. When the royalty abandoned her, the gangsters relocated up west, and the scallies moved in, she became the tired watering hole of choice for the local crim's. Dan stood outside and shook his head. "Fucking shit hole. Should be bulldozed." Then he remembered it was a useful place to find the type of people he needed now.

He pushed the door open and the seven occupants scattered between the bar and one occupied table, stopped their conversations and turned towards him. As soon as they recognised the face they turned back to their previous group. All except the two men at the table. They nodded to Dan and he crossed the room and sat down. "Nice place," he said.

"It's our local," said the fatter one of the two. By fatter, Dan thought it was all about perspective. Either one would have qualified as walking heart attack material but, if you were laying a bet at the bookies next door, you would have picked the one who was struggling to breath while sitting.

"You lost some weight Ricky?" said Dan.

"Yeah I have. Glad you noticed Dan.

"What did you do, cut your toenails you fat twat?"

Ricky's smile disappeared and he remembered how much of a miserable shit Dan was.

"What do you want Dan, because if it's a date, you can fuck right off?"

Dan was getting more pissed off. Until recently, no one would even look at him sideways without getting a good slap. Now, since Sean had arrived, everyone thought they could take the piss, and Dan's piss was now exhausted. "Ricky, if you ever flap that smart mouth in front of me again I will fucking remove it from your head!" His voice was loud enough to get the attention of the closest group and he realised this wasn't the time to be conspicuous, so he lowered it again. "I have a very simple job for you that will make you a monkey each."

"£500 for what?" said Ricky's mate.

"To have a beer at my expense in the Angel."

"But that's full of gavvers!"

"Yes I know, that's the point. I need you to have a conversation surrounded by off duty coppers."

"What conversation?"

"I want you to go to the pub tonight. It will be busy between nine and ten. Act like a couple of drunk pricks. That shouldn't be hard for you two. I want you to start talking about that stolen artwork, you know, the big job on that property developers house up west.

"Richard somebody wasn't it?"

"That's it, something like that anyway."

"I want you to say something like this to each other. You've heard that the Picasso is stashed at Sean O'Shea's mother's house and that he stashed it there. Make sure they hear Picasso and Sean's name."

Both men looked like they had been handed a live rattle snake. "Are you fucking kidding Dan? Sean will go mad and if he knows we've done him over, he'll kill us! They said that job was worth over…"

Dan cut him off. "I know what it was worth. I also know Sean won't do a thing because he will be banged up permanently."

"We want an Archer… …each."

Dan looked at the shabby unshaven fuck wits across the table. "If I give you four grand you better get it done and after it's done bugger off out of town for a few days. Here's an extra monkey for expenses. Just remember, if you fuck it up I will come looking for you and Sean's not the only dangerous one in our family." Dan pushed an envelope between their pint glasses.

"Why do you want Sean tucked up? He's your family."

Dan stared back with black eyes and a closed mouth.

"Ok Dan, it's your tin you are spending. We'll text you when it's done."

"Good," he said standing up.

"Dan?" said the smaller of the two.

"What?"

"You going to a funeral?"

The Irishman looked down at his black suit and tie. "Yes lads, as a matter of fact I'm going to Sean's dads funeral but if you don't do this right, I'll be going to two more tomorrow. Now fuck off and be at the Angel at 9pm."

As Dan walked through the bar and onto the street Ricky looked at his mate. "That, my friend, is one mental bastard. We must be fucking crazy to get involved with him." Then he picked up the money, stuck it in his jacket pocket and phoned for a black cab to go to the Angel at 8:30 that night.

Audrey had been sitting in her kitchen with May and a whiskey and ginger since mid morning. It was Mays tipple of choice and she had decided Audrey needed something to help face the funeral. In the living room, a steady stream of relatives had been met by Bill. Each asked the same question. "Where's Sean and Dan?"

"Dan's told me he had to sort out a little business before he headed over and Sean is on his way." He lied. Bill had no idea where Sean was or if he was coming at all. In fact he didn't know if either of Ray's kids were going to the funeral. Theresa had locked her door and wouldn't come out.

The front door opened and Sean walked in dressed in a black suit. He nodded to Bill and walked straight up the stairs. At his sisters door, he tapped quietly and, after a few seconds, the lock clicked. He opened the door and walked in.

Theresa was still in her dressing gown. "Not ready yet sis?"

"I can't go Sean."

"Yes you can. I don't want to be there either, apart from to dance on his grave, but mum needs us with her."

"Sean, you don't know…"

He walked over and put his arms around her as she stopped mid sentence.

"I know Theresa."

She jumped back. "But…"

"The day you took the overdose." He hugged her again and put his mouth next to her ear. "I killed him. I blew his shitty rapist head off Theresa."

She started sobbing uncontrollably but managed to hug him as tight as a bear. "Thank you," she said and kissed him on the cheek.

"Ok, now we need to support mum and enjoy watching that sick fuck get lowered into the ground so go get dressed treacle."

She managed a weak smile, picked a dress out of the wardrobe and closed the bathroom door behind her.

Twenty minutes later they walked down the stairs together and headed for the kitchen. As they entered, Audrey looked up. She managed the same weak smile her daughter had, lifted the tumbler and downed her drink. She stood up and the three held hands in a circle. "Let's make certain he gets buried and we can get on with our lives once and for all," she said. They broke up and walked to the living room and started shaking hands and being polite.

As Sean got close, Bill pulled him to one side. "Im glad you are going to the funeral Sean."

"It's not for him Bill. It's for mum. That fucker was a sick bastard and he wasn't even my dad."

Bill stepped back like Sean had punched him in the gut. "What? What do you mean?"

"You heard me. He killed my dad, whoever that was, and took his place."

"Look Sean, this isn't the time. I'll come over and see you tonight."

Outside the cortege rolled to a stop and the room slowly emptied. Sean was last out of the door. He looked around the room. "This place needs to go. Mum was right, they both needed a new start," and he closed the door behind him.

By the time Bill knocked on the apartment door it was already dark outside. He put a hand on Sean's shoulder as he walked in. "Put the kettle on lad."

"Come on old man, let's go into the kitchen."

"Old man? You cheeky shit." It didn't matter how much bravado Bill had, it was obvious to them both that life was catching up with him fast. When Sean had first returned he was shocked at how his uncle was showing the years, but now, after the strain of the last few weeks, Bill was shrinking more every day.

It still didn't stop him sounding like the head of the family though. "How's things? You've had quite an ordeal but I'm glad you were at the funeral with your mother."

"I did what I had to do, and that's that." His face darkened. "But you've got a bloody nerve after all the shit you've caused, keeping me in the dark about this as well as Tasha."

Bill opened his mouth to speak but Ami walked in.

"Hi, Bill!" She was genuinely glad to see the old guy and kissed him on the cheek. "Sorry, I've got to dash. See you later, Sean. I'm off to work for my last shift. Can't wait until we get away tomorrow! See ya, babe!"

Sean looked alarmed, hearing Ami mention the holiday in front of Bill caught him off guard.

Bill looked at Sean and them back to Ami. "How's things?"

"I'm OK."

"Listen, I heard what Dan did and I'm sorry. Take this and buy something nice to wear for your holiday. Have a nice time." He palmed a roll of fifty pound notes into her hand.

"Bill that's not necessary…"

"My treat sweetheart. It will make an old man

happy."

She looked over his shoulder at Sean. The big guy nodded and she kissed Bill on the cheek again, waved bye and left them alone.

"She's a lovely girl, isn't she?

"Very special. We get on so well. Dan shouldn't have touched her."

Bill looked at the ground. Even after the life he lived, Sean appreciated the old man could still feel shame.

"No he shouldn't have. He can be a prat sometimes."

"Only sometimes?"

"Sean, I wish you two could just get on. Families shouldn't be like this…   …Christ. We're in business together, for God's sake!

"Tell him, not me. The drugs don't help. He's never straight. His brain's fucked anyway and being high doesn't help."

"Don't say that... I know I need to deal with him and I will, Sean…   …I promise."

Sean turned to face the window. "Look, I've been thinking. Ami's in my life now and I don't want this shit anymore. The Dan stuff, looking over my shoulder the whole bloody time. Ami doesn't need that sort of life."

As he looked at the back of his young nephews head the penny dropped with the sound of truck crash. "No! I'm not bloody hearing this! No fucking way, Sean! Don't start that again. You are only just back. Number one. In a few months you'll be untouchable. We all will."

"I know, but I didn't know it would be like this." He turned around and looked Bill in the eyes. "I want out and that's that." In front of him the disappointment turned to rage.

"No! If word gets out, you'll be fucking dead in a day Sean. You've made too many enemies and the only thing keeping the sharks from eating you alive is having the family behind you. Dan will use this to cut you out. He'll say you are a loose cannon and are walking off with enough information to hang us all. And what about the IRA?"

"I'm family, for fuck's sake! I can be trusted, you know that!"

"Come on, Sean. You know it's not down to me. My time is nearly up. You were lucky last time. I could protect you, but now? Things are very different. Our other business partners won't let anyone walk. I'm in as deep as you. Come on, you must know that?"

"What is it with you lately? You're no help, no fucking help whatsoever! I'm so fed up with all of this and the secrets, fucking secrets all the time!"

"What are you talking about?"

"You won't tell me who my real father was, and don't say you don't know 'cause I know you Bill, and I know when you're hiding something. Just go! Go on! Close the door behind you."

Bill walked down the hall. For a second he turned to talk but stopped himself and let himself out.

About ten minutes later the buzzer rang.

Sean lit up. The old man had changed his mind. At last some answers.

"Hello," he said into the intercom.

Serj's voice sounded quiet. "Come downstairs, I've got something for you."

"Not a good time Serj."

"Stop fucking around Sean. Get your tweeds on

and get down here now."

It was unlike Serj to bark at him. It must be important so he pulled on some boots, grabbed his jacket off the hook and made his way to the elevator.

At the main door Serj was nowhere to be seen. Then, over the top of a hedge at the end of the building, a hand waved and his friends head popped over the top. As Sean rounded the corner his mate said, "Got you a present'" and opened the boot of the car. As he got close it was obvious someone was inside. There was just enough light to make out Gary Dolan, bloodied, tied and terrified.

"What the fuck is Dolan doing jammed in the back of your car Serj. I told you to keep an eye on Dan."

"I did but after you shot Dan I hadn't got anyone else to follow. Well, apart from this turd."

"But why him?"

"Because, just before you ventilated your cousin, the two of them were looking very cosy at your club."

Sean looked down at the, now wide eyed, Dolan. "Really? Dan you sneaky traitorous little shit working with Gary Dolan." He looked back at his friend. "I suppose you asked our friend here what they were up to?" Based on the amount of blood covering the man in the car, Serj had asked him a lot.

"What you would be more interested in to start with is where I picked him up. He and two of his crew were at your mum's house."

Gary tried to slide further back into the boot. In front of him, Sean's face had grown horns and fangs.

"Stupid fucking prick. What was he doing at my mum's?"

"He and Dan had cooked up a scam to frame you for an art robbery. Right now there is a Picasso in your mum's loft and some mates of Dan's are trying to drop you in the clag with the coppers at the Angel."

The irishman looked at his watch. "We have got time to nip around to the house and grab it before they turn up mob handed."

Serj slammed the trunk closed and sat on the edge. "We could, or we could have some other fun."

"Such as?"

"Might I suggest that, now we know, it's a good time to get even. Teach your Dan a lesson?"

"Ok. I'm in. What about your best friend in the car?"

Serj just shrugged his shoulders.

"Fine, I'll leave the details to you but make certain nothing comes back to us."

"No problems. I suggest you wait at the club. It will be the first place the police will look for you."

The two men shook hands and walked in opposite directions. Serj's car roared into life and Sean pulled a phone out of his pocket. "Slippery?"

"Hello Sean."

"Are you busy later tonight?"

"I can free up my schedule if needed my boy. What had you in mind?"

"I thought I would get myself arrested for art theft, handling stolen goods plus breaking and entering."

"You are a busy boy Sean. Tell me the details."

As he walked to the car, Sean explained what he had in mind. By the time he reached for his keys he had finished the call. Now he pointed the 4x4 toward Soho and 8ish. "Dan, you greasy arsehole, karma's coming for you and she's driving a fucking tank."

It was 11pm and Audrey and her daughter were just

about to go to bed when a knock on the door surprised them both. Theresa called through the door "Who is it?"

"Good evening Theresa, it's Patrick Shawcross. I just popped around for a tea."

Theresa looked behind her and called to her mum. "It's Slippery. He wants a tea."

Audrey walked into the hall. "Patrick?"

"Yes my dear, I know it's late but I think it would be a good idea if you let me in and put the kettle on. You will have some visitors very soon."

Audrey nodded to her daughter and Theresa opened the door.

"Thank you my dear, now lets get that kettle on. I need a chat before the police arrive. We may only have a short time."

Slippery sat in front of them explaining that the Dolan's were trying to fit Sean up for a robbery. He omitted the part where Dan was involved and asked them if they ever went into the loft.

"No, only Ray ever went up there."

"Perfect, only his prints will be found. Now, the only place the trail will lead is to a dead man. Are you ok with that?"

The two women looked at each other and grinned. "Absolutely," they said in unison.

At that moment there was a loud bang at the door. "Police, open up!"

"I'll get this ladies, you make the tea. One sugar for me please."

Patrick "Slippery" Shawcross got to his feet, opened the door and said "Good evening, D.I. Holmes. What a surprise seeing you at this late hour."

Holmes looked at the man dressed from head to

foot in tweed. "Fuck me, Slippery Shawcross."

I probably will D.I. Holmes but before we get into the details, do you take sugar in your tea?"

By the time a dozen uniformed men burst through the door of the club, Sean made certain he had a good meal washed down with a Guinness or two. It would be unlikely he would get anything to eat in the cells.

Dan had been watching from the other side of the bar, confused as to why his cousin was stuffing himself at two in the morning.

"Sean O'Shea, you are under arrest for theft."

Dan folded his arms, pleased with how things were panning out. As Sean was cuffed and led out, his cousin waved bye bye. Sean grinned from ear to ear.

Dan stopped waving. Why was he so bloody happy? Something wasn't right.

Karl had had a heavy night. He had arrived home shortly after he watched the club fill with coppers. To start off, he thought it might be a drugs raid and that he might get caught up in it. Then they dragged Sean away in handcuffs. "Good riddance," he thought but left the club just in case. By the time he got back to his flat Tasha was completely wasted on booze and coke. She was passed out on his bed with empty baggies beside her. "Not long now sweetheart. Soon be time to get you into the good stuff."

He fished in his pocket and found one bag left. "Shame to waste it," he said and tipped it onto the table. He cut it into lines and snorted them all. An open bottle of Black Jack was on the floor. Karl picked it up and sunk a few swigs. In minutes he was flying.

By the time he woke up the next morning Tasha was looking in his pockets.

"What the fuck are you after?"

"I need some Charly baby. I'm having a bad start to the day."

"You know this stuff won't be free for ever don't you. Everyone has to pay sometime, one way or another."

"I can pay in kind," she said slipping her shirt off her shoulder and fluttering her eyelashes.

"Wait there," he said.

Inside the kitchen he closed the door. He pulled on one of the draws in the main wall unit. It slid forward until it hit the stops. With a little effort he lifted the front and it came free off the rails. Karl always made certain to keep his stash hidden, especially with a junkie in the flat. As he turned the drawer onto its face he expected to find a large white packet taped to the back end.

Nothing.

Panic set in. Maybe it fell off and was stuck in the carcass. He began pulling more drawers until every one was on the floor. Where the fuck had it gone? Then he spun around and tore through the door. "Where is it you bitch?"

Tasha looked shocked as he pinned her on the bed. "Where is it? That's a months worth of stock and it's not paid for yet. So where is it!" He slapped her across the face.

Tasha started crying, "I don't know what you are talking about?"

"If I cannot pay for that key I'm a fucking dead man!"

"I don't…"

Karl slapped her again before she could finish. "You are just as fucked up as your shitty dad. That's why he won't be out of the joint this time."

His phone pinged as a message flashed onto the screen. It said, "Need to meet at mine now. Dan"

"Don't leave this flat you slag or they will be dragging you out of the Thames in the morning. I've got to go out."

He slammed the door and left Tasha curled in a ball holding her face and crying.

Maddy had spent the morning restocking the bar and running a stock take on the spirits. Since she started, the glamour of working in 8ish had worn thin. Yes, she had made some good connections and been taken to a couple of ccleb parties but the downside was running a business like this was hard work for everyone especially the staff. Today was worse than normal. Dan had limped in early after the previous night's craziness. He had spent thirty minutes winding himself tighter than a broken cuckoo clock. "Maddy, he screamed from the office. "Have you seen my fucking phone?"

"What's it look like Dan?"

His head popped around the office door. "Like a fucking hat. What the bloody hell do you think it looks like? A fucking phone you stupid tart, it looks like a fucking phone."

"Where did you see it last?"

"If I knew that I wouldn't be asking where my phone was. I'd be picking it up and going, *there's my phone, exactly where I saw it last,* wouldn't I?"

"I just meant, where did you last use it?"

"I could have sworn I had it when I left the club

last night but I turned my flat upside down this morning and nothing."

"Do you have your Apple log in password?"

"Yeah, why?"

Maddy pulled out her phone and opened a web browser. She typed in the Apple website and clicked login. "Here, log in and then go to Find My iPhone."

Dan did as he was told. As soon as he selected the device a map appeared. In the middle was a small dot. It was right over his flat. "Bollocks, it must be there after all."

"If you log into your computer at home you can get it to make a sound so that you can find it even if its on silent."

After a begrudging "Thanks," he headed back to the car to go pick it up.

Karl had arrived at the apartment and texted that he was outside the door. The buzzer sounded signifying the catch had been opened remotely.

He walked to the lift, pressed the button and climbed in. At the top floor the doors opened and he walked to the only door on that level. "How the other half fucking live," he thought. The door was ajar and he knocked and walked in.

After closing it he walked through to the kitchen calling Dan's name. As he entered the room he heard a click from behind him. Serj stepped into the room. "I'm sorry, Dan's not home right now but we can have a chat while we are waiting."

Karl started backing away slowly as the barrel of a silenced 9mm swung towards his head. "Who the fuck are you."

"I'm a singing telegram."

"What the fuck?"

Serj started rapping to a familiar chart beat. "Karl keeps Tasha's head in a bag of blow, Karl needs to go."

"Tasha? She's nothing to do with me."

Serj ignored him and carried on rapping. "Karl keeps Tasha down on her luck, Sean sends a message, Karl is fucked!"

"Sean? No…"

"Night fucking night you scum," said Serj and raised the gun to Karl's head.

In the interview room, Slippery sat next to Sean. The door opened and D.I. Holmes walked in flanked by a sergeant. He sat down, pulled out some papers and shuffled them in front of him.

"So Sean, are we going to waste time or are you going to explain why we found a stolen painting hidden in your mothers loft and the word on the street is that you stole it."

Sean leaned back in his chair. "Over to you Patrick."

Slippery stared across the table. "Officers, the way I see it and I'm sure the CPS will view this in the same light, you have nothing on my client. Yes, you found the stolen property at his mother's house, but not at his home. This does not mean it has anything to do with my client."

Sergeant Adamicz leaned forward. "Don't piss around. We have information that Sean has been involved in this crime."

"I suppose those witnesses have made statements and are willing to go to court?"

The sergeant immediately leaned back. "We are actively locating them right now, and as soon as we do your client is stuffed, so why don't you just save everyone else some time."

Slippery smiled. Both officers hated it when Slippery smiled.

"Gentlemen, you have no witnesses? No written statements against my client? No fingerprints of his in the loft."

Holmes looked startled. "How did you know that?"

"Because my client has never been in that loft. I will guess that the only prints you have found are the ones of a Ray O'Shea, a known local criminal. Unfortunately Mr O'Shea died after the robbery was performed so we have no way of knowing why he stole the picture and hid it, unknown to any of his other family members, in the loft of his house." He closed the folder in front of him. "Therefore, officers I suggest you have nothing but hearsay. There is no actual proof this is linked to my client whatsoever and all you have done is cause him embarrassment and wasted a day of his life. Your superiors will, of course, be hearing about this."

As if on cue, the desk phone rang. Holmes picked it up. "Yes sir. I am interviewing him now. No Sir. His fathers prints." He became increasingly uncomfortable. "No sir, we are still trying to locate them. They seem to have left town." After a long pause he said "Yes sir."

He placed the phone back in the cradle. "You can go."

The sergeant looked shocked. "But boss…"

"Show Mr O'Shea and Mr Shawcross to the front desk."

Sean leant forward. "Quick question lads, what's the time?"

"It's 12:34," said Holmes and clicked the button to

stop the recoding of the interview.

Twenty minutes earlier, Dan parked in the reserved space outside his apartment. He had lived there for five years and enjoyed the exclusive postcode it enjoyed. Not many people his age could afford the whole top floor of one the most famous buildings in London. After locking the Mercedes, he buzzed himself through the door and headed up to the apartment.

As soon as he entered he headed straight to the small office set up next to the living room. A large silver Apple Mac sat in the middle of his desk. Within seconds, a larger version of the map Maddy had shown him, was filling the screen. A button told him he could send a signal which would make the phone ring. He clicked go.

Two rooms away a faint sound filled the air. He got up and started following it. Dan walked through the bedroom and stopped at the door to the bathroom. The phone was warbling away inside. "Must have left it next to the crapper," he said and stepped into the room. Karl was laying in the bath with two holes in his forehead and most of his brains all over the wall. On the floor was a key of cocaine which had split, spilling half its contents on the tiles. Just between him and the coke was a gun, his gun from the bedroom drawer. "What the fuck?"

A loud bang from the hall made him panic. He grabbed the gun and made his way to the door.

"Police, open up!" shouted a voice just outside. Before he could move the door exploded inwards and armed cops filled the hallway all pointing guns and shouting instructions. Dan dropped the gun and within seconds his face was pressed to the floor and his wrists were in handcuffs.

From way back in the apartment a voice shouted, "Sarge, you are not going to fucking believe this."

After a few minutes an officers face appeared beside him. "Dan, you fucking piece of shit, you are nicked my man. I would take a long look at this place before you leave. I have a feeling you won't see it again.

TWELVE

Over the last twenty years, London had become the second most surveyed city on Earth, only surpassed by Beijing. At any one time, half a million cameras are capturing peoples movements around the city. With one exception. On the Isle of Dogs, in East London, near Millwall Park, there are several roads to the river. One dead ends in a car park at the bank. Although there are several CCTV cameras, none face the entrance or the wall at the river.

Serj had found this place a year earlier and it had served him well.

As he backed his car to the edge, the rear tailgate made it easy to get the contents of his boot over the wall. He pushed the large sack to the edge. It had been carefully weighted to keep it on the bottom but not anchor it in place. The ebb tide had started to pick up and would soon be running at 8mph. By the time there was light in the sky, the corpse would be in the estuary and heading out to sea.

As soon as it hit the water he closed the tailgate. "Nice evening for a swim," he thought and headed back to town. On the way in he phoned Sean. "Meet in ten minutes?"

"Yeah, at the cafe on the green."

"No probs," said Serj and a few minutes later the two were sitting in his car together.

"How's it going Sean?" said Serj.

"It's going so well it's gone my friend."

"Why, what's so good?"

"By the time I made it back to my apartment, D.I .Holmes was already there. He must have left the station minutes after me.

"What did he want?"

"Apparently, Dan had been screaming blue murder after they arrested him. He said I set him up for Karl's murder and the drug bust."

"How did that conversation end?"

"I asked the copper when the killing took place. It turns out, it was while he was interrogating me. He is my alibi."

"I bet that went down well."

"Yeah, not so much. He was pretty pissed when he realised what had happened. By the way, where is Gary?"

Serj looked east as if they should both be able to see where the senior Dolan had ended up.

"I have bad news Sean, Gary committed suicide."

Sean looked in the same direction. "Unfortunate. How exactly did he do that?"

"Well it was a bit of a mess. According to reports, he shot himself in the back of the head twice, drove to the Thames and drowned himself in a weighted sack."

"Fuck me Serj, he wasn't taking any chances."

"*Better safe than sorry* was his motto at the end Sean."

"D.I. Holmes said he was actively looking for two men that had information regarding my involvement in an art robbery."

"Yes, I had heard the same. If he decided to look in the skip two doors down from his house, he might find what's left of them."

Sean looked away from the river and back at his friend. "Are you serious?"

"*Repay no one evil for evil, but give thought to do what is honourable in the sight of all. Romans 12:17-21.*"

"I love that you are a good catholic like my family Serj, but an honourable end is not being cut into pieces and dumped in a skip. The end of the bible quote is *Beloved, never avenge yourselves, but leave it to the wrath of God.*"

"Ah, but you have to remember Sean, I am only half catholic on my mums side so I only learnt half of it. Anyway, I like my half better than the rest. Those dirty shite's won't rat out anyone else for a wedge of cash."

"No problems with me Serj. Just glad you are here to help."

Serj looked at his old friend. "Sean, my sister is alive and living a good life because of you. You found the two of us when we were at the bottom of a huge shit hole."

"Piss off Serj. You owe me nothing. Happy to help."

"And so am I, at least you are in the clear now."

Sean looked down at the dashboard. "Not by a long shot and you need to keep away from me as of now."

"Sean, Dan's fucked. He's got no cards to play and couldn't bluff his way out of a clogged up urinal."

"I told Bill I want out."

"Good, he's too old to get involved now."

"You forget our history. We made our money in the 80's supporting the cause."

"The IRA are ghosts. Who cares now?"

"Serj, there are a lot of people who could still end up in prison or dead if I spilled my guts. They aren't going to want me out there ticking like a time-bomb. If Bill doesn't tell them, Dan will."

The man in the passenger seat reached behind him and pulled out a matt grey cannon. Sean guessed it was a .44.

"This, my friend takes one of the most powerful

shells ever made and will cut through steel like warm butter. If anyone sticks a gun in your face it will relocate their head to the moon."

Sean took the gun, "Yeah, but this isn't going to keep me alive. These men make Dan look like a sardine in the food chain."

"Go on holiday. Get some sun. Relax. I'll work on a plan to get you both out of the country permanently. Somewhere the Irish can't get to you."

Serj climbed out of the car and walked back to his own.

The big Irishman stared down at the magnum in his hand. He pointed it at the world in front of him and felt the weight. "Empty," he thought. He imagined every problem he had was square in the sights and pulled the trigger. A loud clack echoed in the car. "If you want me dead you are going to have to bleed for it you fuckers." His hand felt the seat where Serj had sat. As expected, a heavy box of jacketed cartridges was waiting. He pulled six free, loaded the cylinder and pushed it back in place. As it locked he caught his reflection in the mirror. "Time to fight for the life you want."

Her Majesty's Prison Belmarsh opened in 1991 on disused land that later became the home of the 2012 Olympic Games. It is a shit hole. A giant rat run full of the worst criminals in the UK. Rapists, murderers and terrorists.

To survive in the modern equivalent of a dungeon you have to be either as hard as granite or connected. Dan had lived his life under the protective umbrella of the O'Shea family name. That sun was now setting.

Bill had owned the prisons in the UK for forty

years. Every prisoner or IRA inmate. Every screw, warden or governor.

And now Dan was the king of the toilet. The shit king Emperor of the building. But no one knew it. His family had lived on its reputation and the links with the IRA but those days were gone. Only Sean had been able to rebuild some of the legend but Dan didn't live in his cousins protective shadow. Quite the opposite. He had made an enemy of the only person who could buy him some favours inside.

Now Dan had two separate problems. First and foremost was how to survive in one of the toughest prisons in England. Second, how could he reach out to take revenge on Sean. His life had been on the ascension before that bastard had limped back to the family and kiss his dad's arse. Worse than that, his dad had just dropped his trousers and let his cousin fuck him yet again while he chose Sean in favour of his own boy.

Dan stared at the door of the visitation room. Around him were a dozen other inmates talking to family and friends. The door opened and Bill walked in. He slowly made his way to his sons table and sat down.

"It's been a long while since I sat in one of these. Still smells the same," said Bill. "How's it going son?"

"I don't know dad, I've been left in here to fucking rot! When's Slippery going to work his magic and get me home?"

"It's not that easy, son. You'll have to be patient, they've got you bang to rights, but I'm working on it."

Dan slammed his hand on the table. "Patient, dad? Jesus! I've been fucking fitted up and you expect me to be patient? You're having a laugh, ain't yah?"

"Fitted up? Come on Dan. You are always as high as a kite, you probably can't remember..."

"Don't be ridiculous! Of course I'd remember! They found 60-bloody-k of coke. Don't you think I'd remember that?"

"Sean gets fitted up and blames you and now you do the same. This can't be right."

"Oh, I see. Now, I get it! Fucking Sean's done this!"

"Don't be bloody stupid! That's not what I was saying. If anything it would have been the Dolans. Gary's gone missing. Who knows. Sean wouldn't do this to you!"

Dan stood up. "That's it! It would never be the perfect fucking Sean! It never is, is it?" He stepped back and turned away. "Fuck off, dad! Just fuck off and play happy families with that bastard! I'm outta your way now! You never back me."

Two officers walked over and stepped between the two men. "You ok Mr O'Shea?"

Bill turned to the uniforms. Yeah we are good thanks." They walked away. "Dan, for Christ's sake, grow up! I've got Sean in one ear moaning about you and wanting out again and now you banged up in here. I shouldn't be going through all this shit at my age. You're both grown ups!"

"Hang on, he's fucking what? He's trying to get out! Again?"

Dan grabbed his chair and launched it across the room at Bill. Within seconds the guards drop him to the ground and pin him on his stomach. Another drags Bill away.

"Dan, it's got to stop! All this... ...please! Look, I'm doing my best to get you out. We're trying everything son." The guard dragged him back but the old man suddenly became a dead weight. In a second he had dropped to his knees holding his arm. After coughing hard he raised his head and watched his son being dragged back into population.

"Dan!"shouted his dad as he collapsed onto the floor in the middle of the room.

"Mr O'Shea, are you ok?" said the guard.

"Help me to the door. I need you to call my driver."

"Where do you want to go when I call him?"

"Just say I want to see Slippery, he'll know what I mean."Bill staggered to his feet and allowed the officer to walk him to the door. He needed to get Dan out of here. He knew his son wasn't built to survive this place on his own.

Slippery's office had seen better days and worse days.Originally above a jeans wholesaler in Whitechapel, it had eventually made it to a corner site occupying a second rate postcode in Cheapside near to where the Barings Brothers, had started their bank 200 years earlier. When Nick Leeson crashed the bank in 1995 with debts of $1.4 Billion, he took a slice out of Patricks hard stolen nest egg and caused him to move one last time. Now he was back close to where he had started out. In a side street adjacent to the Barbican, Shawcross and Steel had taken residence in the top floor for the past ten years. Patrick liked his silent partner, James Steel. When things got difficult with various official agencies James was the person who was listed as the responsible party from a legal standpoint. The fact that James, for all intents and purposes, had left England to reside in the Cayman Islands ten years earlier made it very difficult to pin him down to ask questions. What made it even more difficult was the fact that James Micheal Steel had died at the age of 5 and his identity was now a complete fabrication that enabled Slippery to distance himself from many shadowy connections. This made Steel the best partner a brief for the O'Sheas could have.

Steel had 23 clients according to their books and in the last decade had managed to lose money on all of them, particularly through pro-bono and charitable work. In reality, Shawcross and Steel had only one client, Bill O'Shea and now he was striding through reception past the bemused temp working at the front desk.

"Excuse me, sir! You can't just barge in! Mr. Shawcross is with a client."

Bill ignored her and carried on into the office and she ran behind him.

Inside the office Patrick was sitting at his desk with his trousers around his ankles. Kneeling in front of him was a slightly plump girl who was busy earning her rent for the week.

"Bill," said Patrick, "please take a seat." He stood up, pulled his trousers back around his waist and fastened his belt. Shannon sweetheart, can we pick this up tomorrow, I think I will be busy for the remainder of the day my love."

The girl at his feet stood up straightened her dress and breezed past the bemused receptionist. "Sophie my dear, this is a very important client. Please make certain you ask him if he would like a coffee."

"Would you like a coffee?" said the girl still trying to get her head around seeing a potential client on her knees with her bosses penis in her mouth.

Bill looked behind him. "Tea with milk and two please."

"And can you be a dear and get me an espresso as well. Thank you Sophie."

"Patrick, I need to see you now."

"I'm always here for you Bill. Now, what's the problem, and I am going to guess it has something to do with Dan."

"I've just been to see him and he's in a state. You need to find a loophole, something, no matter what it takes. Just get him out." Bill slumped into a chair and gasped for air.

"Bill?" said Slippery, concerned for his old friend. The old man waved him away as if to say it wasn't important.

"Look Bill, there's nothing I can do this time. I've tried every conceivable way. What doesn't help is the fact that Dan and Sean hate each other. You know they are making this worse for themselves, don't you?"

"Don't be stupid. This is someone from the outside fitting them up. Probably the Dolans."

Patrick looked at his friend puzzled. Bill was one of the smartest men he knew. How could he be so blind to what was going on?

"Look, I'm on it. I'm not just leaving him to rot inside, you know? If anything new emerges I'll do the best I can but, as it stands, they have Dan legally stuffed. Unless, of course you have him sprung?"

"That would be the last resort. If nothing else works, that's my final move."

Bill, I'll come and see you later at the club. Let's talk then.

"8ish?" He said looking down. The brief had his flies still open.

"Patrick, you are a dirty old man but I trust you. Help Dan out. He's not Sean. He can't handle a long stretch."

"Later Bill, I'll do what I can. For you my friend."

He stood up, zipped up his flies and shook hands. "Bill?"

"Yes Slippery."

"It's not going to end well, you do know that don't you?"

Bill didn't answer but pulled the door open and then let it slam behind him.

THIRTEEN

Dan had been pacing in his cell for an hour. Apart from a visit from a screw to take some coke off him for a bribe to keep him away from some of the psychos in his wing he hadn't seen anyone all morning.

Every time he passed the back wall he slammed his weight against the rear post of his bunk. It caused a satisfying clang against the wall and made him feel as if he was in control of a small part of his restricted world. Deep inside he knew it was bullshit. He was scared most of the time he was awake or asleep. Outside, he had a small army who jumped every time he spoke. Here, he had no-one. His dad's influence didn't reach this far now he'd grown old. Ironically, Sean was the only one who could make it easy for him in here but he knew that wouldn't happen. In fact, his cousin had the ability to reach in and have him killed at anytime. Dan looked in the mirror. "Fucking Sean. This isn't fair."

The door opened behind him and a guard walked in. "You have a special visitor. Mr Kelly is waiting for you."

"About fucking time."

The officer stepped into Dan's face. "Let me be very clear O'Shea, you better be respectful when you see him. If you shoot your mouth off you won't last the day. Understand you little piece of shit."

Dan looked down, "Ok, I understand."

"Good now get a move on you little turd before I have to motivate you."

In the massive, but empty, visitor room, one man sat at a table on his own. He was a tall, smartly dressed man in his sixties and looked at the window as Dan approached and fell into the chair opposite.

Behind O`Shea the guard waited. After a few seconds the man turned to the officer and said, "Thanks Terry. How are the family?" he said in a heavy Belfast accent.

"All well Mr Kelly thank you."

"Good! Let me know if you need anything," he said and looked back out the window. The guard took the hint and walked to the back of the room out of earshot.

"I fucking hate these places Dan. You know that don't you?"

"Yes but this is important Mr Kelly."

The tall man finally turned his head in the direction of the younger man. "Dan, let me get things off to a good start. You are a useless mental fucker. If you were part of the liberation army I would have had you put down a long time ago. As a matter of respect to your Da and your cousin you are still breathing. That doesn't mean that can't change very quickly. Now I seriously fucking suggest you learn some respect!" The last word was barked so loud the guard looked up and started to step forward. The tall man leaned back in his seat and shook his head and, in response the guard stepped back against the wall and made himself busy watching the opposite wall.

"Sorry Mr Kelly but it's Sean who's the problem. He wants out again."

The older man paused as his expression became stern.

"Are you sure this is true? I would have thought I would have heard this from your father, not from you. And you said on the phone that you being banged up in here is Sean's work?"

"Yes, it's true. My concern is that Sean knows a lot and with his knowledge he shouldn't be allowed to walk away again."

The tall man leaned forward. "Dan you may be an arsehole but you are not a complete idiot I hope. You know no one walks away from the IRA. If this is true, as far as I am concerned, he is not going anywhere. How do you know this?"

"My old man."

"And you call this solidarity I suppose? So, you hate Sean so much that you would grass your father up for keeping this quiet?"

"Yep."

"See, you're no good to us either lad. So, I'm telling you, if this is just another nasty little wind up to fuck your cousin over, I'll have you taken care of in here. Do you get me?"

"It's the truth Mr Kelly, honest."

"You do realise that, apart from me, your father is the only other person that can help you get out of this hell hole? Without us you'd be forgotten. I will deal with Sean. What I don't understand is why your father is protecting him?" He waved to the guard. "Take this little shite back to his cell, I'm finished with him here."

"Don't touch my dad though! It's just Sean, you know that?"

Kelly looked at the officer who looked away and made out he hadn't heard a word.

"Shut your fucking mouth. I'll pretend you didn't just forget who you were talking to. Me taking orders from you is not how this works." He looked at the guard. "Take Dan off to his cell and give him a little reminder who the fuck he's dealing with on the way." Before Dan could react a club sized fist knocked him off the chair and he was dragged to the door.

Behind them Mr Kelly started to weigh up his limited options. Too many secrets. Too many years. Too much to lose.

Sean had to be dealt with and Bill needed to know he was not pleased about his choices.

He climbed to his feet, pulled his jacket back in place and pushed open the unlocked steel door as he left the room.

Tasha had been stoned for two days after she heard about Karl's murder. Then she ran out of drugs and decided to get drunk instead. Now she hadn't any more money and her mum had told her she needed to sober up. Instead she decided to confront Sean. As she fell through the doors of the empty club she started shouting slurred words at the top of her voice.

"Sean! Sean where are you, you useless piece of shit!"

Maddy was cleaning down the bar ready to open in a couple of hours time. "Oi! Enough of that! Get out of here before you get in trouble. Anyway, he's not here. He's abroad on holiday for a couple of weeks."

Tasha snarled at Maddy, "Holiday? Fucking perfect!" she screamed and then turned to exit.

As she stumbled out through the door she fell backwards against the wall and sat down holding her knees to her chest. "Fucking Sean O'Shea. You bastard!" She started sobbing into her hands. "Dad.." she said quietly.

From her left, Serj stepped out of the shadows.

"Hello Tasha. I've been looking for you."

She was surprised and embarrassed at the same time. "Who the fuck are you?"

"I'm a friend of your dad's. He sent me to help you."

"While he is having a great time on holiday with his tart?"

"Yes, while he is away and can't be seen to help you because it would be dangerous for you."

"Dangerous? To me? I'm not important to anyone."

"You are to Sean, now come with me. Lets get you a bath, some clean clothes and a meal while I explain."

Tasha opened her mouth to tell the stranger to get stuffed but she was so defeated she just took his hand and allowed him to lift her weight. He put an arm around her waist and walk her to his car around the corner.

"I hate you O'Shea."

"That's an interesting thank you for taking you to the Bahamas for two weeks of five star luxury."

"And that's the problem you heartless bastard. No one has ever treated me like this in my life. The last two weeks have been the best. A man who worships the ground I walk on. Someone who treats me like a queen and for the first time in my life I feel I can be myself without being taken advantage of. Basically you are a shit and have ruined me for every other man."

"You don't need another man. You're stuck with me treacle."

"Exactly! You are a horrible bastard, now give me a kiss and take me away from paradise, back to the real world."

Sean opened the taxi door, kissed her slowly on the lips and let Ami slide into the back of the cab.

He walked to the other side and sat beside her.

"This is the start Ami. I will clean up my problems and we will be a family." He put his hand on her thigh higher than just a friendly pat. She put her hand on his and slid it higher to the bottom of her skirt.

At the airport, Sean's decision to travel business class paid off as they dodged every queue and were sitting in reclining side by side beds within ninety minutes.

A night flight was a perfect way to spend the next few hours. They would land at dawn and Serj had insisted he would meet them.

Ami drank her third glass of Champagne as she laid her bed flat. They had both decided not to have dinner as they were looking forward to an early breakfast.

"Thanks for the last two weeks Sean. It has been magical. I am still wired from the experience. There is no way I will sleep on the way back."

Sean slid his hand under her blanket. "You just need to get rid of that tension and you will sleep like a baby," he said.

His hand moved across her body. Twenty minutes later she fell asleep exhausted. Her teeth marks were still visible on her hand where she bit hard to keep from making too much noise.

"Bastard," she said as she drifted off to sleep.

In the morning they were woken up with coffee, juice and an english breakfast.

"British Airways, you are bloody marvellous," she said and within an hour the wheels of the jet touched down at Heathrow.

As promised, Serj was waiting at the gate.

"Fuck me! Did you two ever see the sun?" he smiled as Ami blushed.

Both of them were very tanned, but Serj was right.

Everyone else on the flight were two shades darker, mostly because they had spent all day in the sun, unlike these two. Ami and Sean had eaten lunch each day and then taken a bottle of Champagne to the room. They spent all afternoon alternating between bed, balcony and the bottle. In the evening they dressed for dinner and Sean slipped the head waiter a ton at the beginning of the holiday to get a quiet table for two on the edge of the beach each night. Later they swam together before walking back to their villa. Nocturnal living didn't help with their tans.

"Serj, it's lovely to see you but please stop embarrassing my intended."

Ami spun her head. "What do you mean intended?"

"I asked you last night. I said do you want to do this forever. You said yes."

"Was that a proposal?"

"What else do you think it was?"

"Sean, you need to work on your communication skills."

"So is that a no?"

"No you idiot, it's a yes of course."

Serj looked at the two of them. "Thank fuck for that. Now can we get the hell out of here. We need a serious conversation before you get to the car."

"Who's car?"

"Bill's. He's waiting for you with your brief."

"Slippery?"

"I think so. They want to talk to you and I'm not here for obvious reasons. Now let's chat so I can leave before you see them."

The three moved to a small cafe and sat while Serj filled in the gaps while they were away.

As they walked out of the terminal Bill's driver flashed the lights. Sean waved and they walked to the vehicle and loaded the luggage into the boot. As soon as they were in the car it accelerated out to join the traffic.

"See, I said they'd be here 8ish, didn't I?"

Patrick looked at his old friend. "Yes, Bill, you did. But the 8ish I thought you meant was in the evening. Not at the crack of dawn."

Sean looked back from the front passenger seat. "Blimey! You've been waiting since sun up? The bloody delays were awful."

"Yes. We saw you had landed nearly an hour ago. Took you a long time to get your bags."

Sean decided not to take the bait. "So why the welcoming committee? You two got nothing better to do?"

Bill took a deep breath. "Dan's been nicked properly. He's on remand. We can't do anything for him."

"Oh well, he's banged up then. It doesn't surprise me Bill."

Patrick leant forward. "There's nothing I can do for him Sean. Too many drugs worth too much money and a dead dealer in his flat shot with his gun. There's no way back from that."

Bill took over. "They blood tested him and he was under the influence of drugs as well. So, he's fucked Sean!"

The younger man became stone faced. "Hang on, why are you telling me this? Like I would give a shit anyway! Come on, you both know what he's been like. He got out of line with Ami, Bill! That's a step too far, even for your son. If it had been anyone else Bill, you know what I would have done to them?"

Ami could see Bill wasn't happy. "Yeah, but Sean," she said "You still wouldn't want any harm coming to him."

"Look Ami, keep out of it, yeah? You are too nice a person to try and bridge this gap. Bill knows what he would have done in my shoes but I still let it slide out of respect."

"See Bill, you know it's not Sean."

The old man looked at Ami. "No, I don't know that."

Sean looked round again. "Bill, if I had been involved Dan would be floating to France by now."

"What are you saying, Sean? Really? Is this your work? Look me in the eyes and tell me."

Without blinking he deliberately said, "No. Of course not."

With that the car fell silent for the rest of the journey back to Soho.

By the time Sean had dropped Ami back at home, unpacked and showered it was early evening. He called a cab and twenty minutes later he was sitting at the bar of The Dog and Duck on Frith Street. In front of him were two pints of beer.

The sound of the door opening made him look at the reflection from the back bar. Serj had walked in. He moved towards the stool next to him and sat down. Without asking he picked up the second pint and drank half of it. "Needed that mate. Been a busy day."

"But productive Serj. You did good work man. Apparently Dan's proper fucked"

"When someone upsets me or my friends they

don't get away with it. Not even if it's your family."

"He's no family of mine. Dan made certain of that when he went after Ami. Now he's just a rabid dog that needs putting down."

Serj looked across at the big Irishman. "There is more Sean. Unfortunately more shit from your man Dan. Rumour has it that he is planning a hit on you by involving the IRA. He has blabbed to your hierarchy that you're getting out again"

Sean turned sharply. "Shit! How'd he know that?"

"This I'm working on. We need to meet in a few days. Until then, you keep your eyes to the ground and your enemies close. Leave the other stuff to me. The only thing you need to get a handle on is your daughter. You need to talk to her. Now!"

"Yeah I know. Is she ready to listen?"

"Maybe. I think yes, but take it easy with her. She's fragile."

Sean picked up his pint, sank it in one and silently walked into the street.

Donna's house was small but respectable, located on an old council estate. Most of the row had been bought by the residents and now there was an air of middle class comfort. Donna's stood out as one of the few that hadn't had quite the same level of care and attention. The style of the door said it had been bought by the owner but the state of the windows suggested money was still an issue.

Sean parked his car at the curb and looked down the street. He grew up close by and knew how hard it was on kids living in this area. In the distance three late teenage boys had grabbed a smaller kid and pushed him up against the wall. One of them was talking and he obviously didn't get the answer he expected. In a flash of anger he lashed out and punched the little boy in the face. For an instant he imagined it was Tasha being bullied. He swung the door wide and stormed over. As he got level with them he shoved the head of the mouthy kid which connected with the other two in a satisfying clacking sound.

"Fuck you cowards!" he barked as the three of them rounded on him.

Mouthy pulled an eight inch fixed blade knife out of his pocket. "I'll fucking kill you you old fart! You're dead."

Sean stepped forward, "You know the two most dangerous things about carrying a knife? The obvious one is if someone takes it away from you. Now you have nothing to use as a weapon and the other person can shove it up your arse so far it will pick your nose."

All three took a step back.

"The second problem is if you threaten someone who has a gun," he pulled the left side of his jacket back and the grip of the pistol came into view. All three took another big step back. "You've heard the expression *never bring a knife to a gunfight*. Well you are about to find out why." He looked sideways at the small boy next to him. "What's your name?"

"Mickey," said the small kid still watching the big man with the gun who had just stopped what was about to turn into a nasty beating and robbery.

"My cousins called Mickey. Nice lad." Sean turned towards the other boys. "So you're the big men on this street are you? Well not anymore. If I find you've upset Mickey or anyone on this street I'll come looking for you. Understand?"

The boys started nodding and were backing away.

"Oi! You! Mouthy! Haven't you forgotten something?"

"What?"

"You forgot to give Mickey all the money in your pockets. All of you. And you can leave the knife behind as well."

"Fuck no! No way!"

Sean stepped forward and knocked the knife to the ground. "You think I'm fucking kidding?" He grabbed the boy by the collar and shook him. "You've caught me on a bad day so I suggest you do as you are told before shit goes sideways you little turd."

All three boys threw bundles of notes on the ground.

"You lot have been busy haven't you. Well, not around here anymore now fuck off before you piss your pants." Sean threw mouthy backwards like he was made of tissue paper and the three staggered away.

He turned to the little boy. "Mickey, you need to do two things if you want to live around here. First, if you get any problems from those tossers you knock on that blue door over there and tell the lady you need Sean's help. Understand?" The boy looked down the road and nodded.

"Second you go to Brick Lane and find a gym called Fast Frankie's. You tell him I sent you and he is to teach you how to box. You go there twice a week until you know what you are doing. Ok?"

The boy nodded again.

"Good, now pick up that money and buy your mum some flowers." Mickey bent down, grabbed the money and walked in the opposite direction to the other boys.

As Sean headed back to Donna's house, he thought

back to when he was a kid. Maybe he would have been like Mickey if Bill hadn't taken him under his wing. Ray had been useless as a father. Bill was the one who taught him how to take care of himself. Trained with him at Frankie's. Turned him into the machine he was now. One that could handle most situations.

As he knocked on the door he wished he had been here for Tasha. Maybe he could have made life easier for her and she wouldn't be in the situation she was now.

The door opened and Donna stood in bare feet, jeans and a T-shirt.

"You took your time."

"I've had a lot on.`

"Yeah you always did. She's round the back."

Sean started to step past her but she put her hand on his chest. It was the first time she had touched him since before Tasha was born, but it felt surprisingly comfortable to her.

"She's a tough nut to crack, Sean. Granted it wasn't your fault, but it don't mean she ain't gonna be stubborn about it."

Sean nodded in thanks and then continued to the back garden. He turned the corner and saw Tasha sitting on the back step, smoking a cigarette."

"You know those things will kill you."

Tasha looked up and took a long drag before throwing it away.

"Look Tasha, I know we've got a lot of work to do here, but I'm game, if you are."

Tasha looked over and contemplated what he said.

Your friend Serj is a nice guy. He came and found me. Said you had sent him. Got to me just in time, I was a bit fucked up after they found Karl."

"How are you now?"

"Still a bit fucked up but I haven't taken coke for a week now."

"You know Karl wasn't good for you. You're better off now."

Tasha opened her mouth as if to argue but closed it again. "Actually it's a relief. I was getting messed up and I think he wanted to make it worse. Now my heads straight I can see he kept pushing me. Why would he do that? What would he get out of it?"

Sean remembered seeing him talking to Dan and the way his cousin talked about her.

"I don't know Tasha. Perhaps he was just evil. Either way, he's gone and I'm back."

"And I'm supposed to trust you after all these years."

"You earn trust. All I want is for you to give me a chance."

She didn't say anything but looked down at her shoes.

"Think about it Tasha." Sean walked back through the house and his daughter turned to watch him go.

When Sean got back to the club he had looked forward to a bit of normality. As he pushed the door open he realised that was not going to happen.

"Look, I don't know where Sean is sweetheart. Maybe you should wait outside until he gets here." Maddy gestured towards the entrance. Behind her Mickey started shaking his head.

"On the street?" said Ami.

"Well maybe you would be at home there," said Maddy with a sarcastic smile on her face.

Ami started in "Look you little tart…"

Sean got to them just before his girlfriend became really personal.

"Ami, lets get going. How about lunch? Maddy, wind your neck in before it gets you looking for a new job."

Maddy returned to stocking the shelves and chatting to Mickey as Sean scooped Ami up under his arm and walked her to his car.

"Sean, I don't like the way she looks at you babe. She obviously fancies you."

"Don't be silly. But I do like it when you get jealous. You obviously care. No, I think Mickey is her cup of tea."

"Really Sean? Don't mock me or treat me like a child."

"Never darling, sweet cheeks, hunny buns, cutie pie." He laughed hard as she threw a slap at his face and missed. Let's go for a steak. I fancy a nice bit of rump," he slapped her bum gently, "just like that."

She smiled up at him, "What are you saying, I'm a bloody cow now?"

"No, darling. Now moooove over a bit so I can get to the gearstick."

"Bloody cheek!" She thumped Sean on the arm so hard it would leave a deep bruise but then rested her hand on his as they drove towards the restaurant.

After lunch, the two stopped at Sean's and spent a couple of hours working off the food they had eaten. By early evening, they were walking back into the club together holding hands.

Suddenly Sean realised someone was approaching from behind.

"Dolan! What are you doing on my ground? You're

the younger brother, yeah?"

"Yes, correct. We need to talk Sean."

Sean put himself between Ami and the young man.

"Darling, go and get yourself a coffee and wait for me in the office." Ami understood the body language and was happy to be away from the confrontation.

The Irishman turned back to Dolan. "You all have the same pig face look about you, don't ya? What do you want?"

"Look Sean. I come in peace. There is a lot of bad blood between our families and I believe most of it is from your cousin Dan and my twat of a brother. Dan's a disgusting piece of filth. We both know he is a fucked up little dick. Did you know what he was doing to your daughter? Karl was spouting shit to everyone. Dan wanted her to start shooting up heroin and end up as a cheap prozzie on the street. He wanted her turning tricks for smack. Dan hates the ground you walk on."

Sean bristled at the thought of his cousin turning his daughter into a prostitute and an addict.

He thought back to seeing Karl and Dan in the club. "You're not wrong there." he said and walked the man to a quiet booth in the corner.

"Sean, I wanna draw a line in the sand and stop this bollocks. I have some information that will mean you owe me one and in return I just want peace. No more killings between us."

"Go on."

"Word has it that your lovely cousin has helped to arrange a hit on you."

Sean controlled himself and pretended he wasn't even fazed. "With who?"

"Your own people. The Irish army"

"You think I should believe you?"

"Believe what you want but it's the truth. I know all this trouble we've had has mostly been down to Dan, my brothers and some informants in our outfit, but they are all fucking poison. We could be a force to be reckoned with if we take the fight outside the families and clean house."

"And what's in it for you?"

"I just want this done. I know one of our men works for Dan but more important I have two sons just like you. Our kids need to be safe don't they?"

Sean thought back to leaving his boys and waving at the window. The thought of them being unprotected made his skin crawl. All this was about getting them back but, if this meant putting them in danger, what was the point?"

"OK. Then you can help me further. Lets talk. I may be living on borrowed time but my girlfriend and kids aren't." Sean put his arm around Dolan's shoulder as they walked to his car, "We need to make room for your crew to take control before I get killed by the Irish, but I need you to promise my Mickey and my family stays safe."

"Likewise Sean."

Ten minutes later, they finished the conversation and after he closed the door to Dolan's car, Sean pulled out his phone and dialled the last number. Serj answered before the second ring.

"What's the game?"

"Serj, I'm a dead man. Ami doesn't know yet and I don't see a way around this. Kelly has put a contract out on me to have me killed."

"Come on Sean. There's always a way."

"Not this time. Dan's done for me but Ami and my

kids are the important ones. I want you to get her, the boys and Tasha out, whatever happens.

"Come on Sean."

"Serj. Do as I'm fucking telling you."

"What do you want me to do?"

"Arrange travel papers and documents for them. Get them away from Kelly and Dan."

"Done."

Sean hung up and walked back into the club.

"Bad fucking timing as always O'Shea. You always run out of time," he said to himself and headed back to find Ami.

"What do you mean I have to leave?" Ami punched Sean for the second time that day but this time she meant it. "You promised me Sean. Forever! You lied to me."

"Ami, you, your daughter, my boys and Tasha will get killed if you stay. It will be a message to anyone who wants out. Its the unwritten rule."

"You have no idea what you have done. I let you in. Why would you do this?"

"Serj will get you out. There is enough money for all of you to live good lives. I made a deal."

"Sean, I don't want money, I want a real life. With you."

"Ami, Serj will look after you. Let's go home. We need to work things out." Sean walked her out to the rear entrance and told her what she needed to do.

As they stepped through the exit, he handed a piece of paper to Ami with Serj's number on it. Phone him when things happen.

The two of them looked up as a black motorcycle engine came to life. The riders jacket was open and his left arm slid inside. As the hand came into view, a long barrel with a suppressor screwed to the end swung up to Sean's chest.

Two 9mm bullets left the barrel with a pop and a hiss.

A muffled voice behind the dark visor said, "Dirty fucking traitor," and then he tucked away the gun and stamped on the gear shift. The rear wheel started spinning and then the front wheel lifted as the tyre caught some traction.

Sean fell to the ground. Ami tried to hold him up but he had stopped breathing before he hit the pavement. "Oh my God! No! Sean, no! Nooo!"

As the rider made it to the end of the road, he glanced in the side mirror. Behind him, a tiny woman was huddled over a big man and was beating on his chest screaming at the top of her voice.

Tasha had been online looking for a job all afternoon. "Mum, do you know anyone at the bookies? Mum? MUM!"

She walked into the living room. "Are you not going to answer me?"

Donna sat with her legs curled under her and a phone cradled in her lap.

"Mum. I'm not invisible."

"Tasha. Your dad's dead."

"Mum, you've said that for years. Give it up."

Donna looked up and fixed a stare at her daughter. "Sean's dead, Tasha."

"WHERE`S MY SON?" Audrey screamed down the corridor. "WHERE?"

A nurse ran over and held her. "Who is your son?"

Slippery stepped past her and talked to the nurse. He had been with Audrey when the police knocked on her door.

"Its Sean O`Shea nurse," said Slippery calmly.

"Sean! Sean ! Where?" Screamed his mum.

The nurse never knew people by their first name but then again she never had someone on her ward that could get her killed.

"He's in here." She pulled Audrey into a side room. On the bed was a semi clothed man with two bullet wounds in his chest and blood all over the sheet.

"Sean, my only boy!"

A Doctor ran into the room. "I'm sorry, the bullets were too exact. He didn't have a chance. Mrs O'Shea? It's your son isn't it?"

"My only son! Please help him." Audrey slumped forward onto the bed.

"He's gone Mrs O`Shea. We couldn't save him. He was gone before he got here. I'm really sorry."

Audrey sat on the bed. Tears streaming down her cheeks.

The doctor was wearing green scrubs but they were spotless. He stepped forward, hugged her tight and said "I'm sorry."

Audrey hugged him back. "What can I do? I can't be here."

"Nurse, please write into the notes, Sean O'Shea has been positively identified. Time of death 18:26."

The nurse wrote in block capitals and then hung the chart on the bed.

"Mrs O'Shea. He's gone now. You should go home." Audrey pushed the door and found Ami on the other side.

"Sean?" said Ami.

Audrey held her hand. "He's gone love. I'm sorry." Then they walked through the swing doors into the waiting room with Patrick just behind them.

Bill stood on the other side. "Audrey?"

She looked deep into his eyes. "We did this Bill. We killed Sean. We put him in the middle of this and he made the only choice he could." She looked at the floor and pushed past him. Slippery followed so that he could drive her back home.

Ami held back. "Bill, I'm sorry."

In forty years Bill hadn't shed a tear. Not after the loss of friends, parents or a brother. As Ami stood in front of him she could see his eyes become glassy.

"Sean loved you Bill. He thought of you as his dad."

"And I loved him too Ami. Like a son."

"Dan made this happen Bill. He told the army Sean was going to leave."

Bill stepped back like he had been punched by a heavyweight. "What the fuck are you talking about Ami?"

"Bill, Sean told me. Dan talked to a man called Kelly." She wiped a tear of her cheek. "Your son started this. Kelly paid money to have Sean killed. Maybe someone got to him first but Kelly had a hit out on Sean. It doesn't matter who killed him. Sean said he was a dead man and wanted to make plans for his family to be safe. The boys, Tasha, Olivia and me."

"Ami, I'm sorry," said Bill. He leant back against the wall and the colour drained out of his face. Inside he felt adrenaline racing through his veins. When he was a young man he would have stormed out on his own. His old body betrayed him. All the anger and vengeance welled up inside but the muscles and flesh couldn't handle it. "Ami…"

"I'm sorry Bill. We all have to take responsibility for this."

She stepped around him as Tasha ran into her.

"Where's my Dad!"

Ami didn't reply. She grabbed Tasha's arm and pulled her through the doors. The young girl started struggling and Ami slapped her hard.

"He's gone. You don't need to see him. Now, come with me. I'll take you home."

Tasha was crying. "I want to see him!"

"Not going to happen. You're going home." Ami dragged her until she was at a black car on the curb. "In!"

Tasha was pushed through the door and after the door closed the car turned in the general direction of Donna's house two miles away.

FOURTEEN

Mr Kelly sat looking at his phone. It had been sitting on the table for twenty minutes completely silent. He took his eyes off it to check his watch and just as he did the phone lit up and started a little vibrating dance on the spot.

The window showed it was a withheld number calling. He picked it up and pressed receive. "You're late."

A voice on the other end said a few words before Kelly went quiet. After ten seconds the voice started talking again.

"Yes," Kelly said. "You'll still get your money." He hung up and put the phone back on the table.

After staring at it for a minute he picked it up and opened up the contacts. After typing B I L, Bills full name came up. He pressed send and the phone started searching for a signal to make the call. The reception was always a nightmare in his kitchen so he turned his head slightly to the right and put the receiver to his ear. On the other end, a small click told him the receiving phone had been answered but before he could say a word a .308 Winchester round with a hollow point tip tore through the window. It hit the back of the phone and began expanding. By the time it entered Kellys head it was the size of a small poker chip and still travelling at over 2000 feet per second. The 175-grain casing it was fired from meant it had started out its flight carrying over 2,600 foot pounds of energy. Although the window and phone had reduced it a little, there was still enough to rip most of his head off and the kinetic energy threw his body sideways onto the floor.

Two hundred yards away, Serj slid the rifle off its makeshift rest. He stood up and melted further into the trees where he laid the gun in the back of his car.

Outside the club, Bill stared at his phone. It had a failed call on the screen with the word Kelly next to it. He tried to return it but the call went straight to answerphone. "Piece of shit." he said out loud meaning both Kelly and the phone.

"Who's that?" said Mickey.

"No one important. Let's get into the club. I want it closed until further notice out of respect for Sean."

As soon as they were inside Mickey told the staff to shut down the sound system. He stood on the nearest table. "Ladies and gentlemen, unfortunately we have had some bad family news. My cousin Sean has died."

In the distance Maddy gasped.

"We will be closing the club as a sign of respect and it will stay closed for the next few days. Now, please finish your drinks and leave as quickly as possible."

Within minutes a steady stream of punters started making their way to the exits but it took nearly two hours to get all of them out, especially with many of the regulars offering their drunken condolences.

Just as the last few were finishing up, D.I. Holmes walked through the door. He spotted Bill and Mickey talking to the staff. As he caught up with them they had finished explaining everyones tasks before they could go home and had then entered the office. Holmes followed them inside.

"Mr O'Shea, I'm sorry to hear about your nephew."

Bill rounded on him, "I bet you are. You and the rest of you pigs will be dancing on his grave. You couldn't wait to get round here and gloat could you"

"That's not why I'm here. I hurried back to London when I heard about the shooting and wanted to ask some questions so that we can find Sean's killer. There is a word out there that some of your Irish friends had put money on his head."

"Don't know what you are talking about."

"Do you know a man called Kelly?"

"No, why should I?"

"We had been told he had a meeting with your son Dan in prison a few days ago."

Bill could feel the anger building in him and his heart started racing out of control. He leaned against the desk for support.

"No idea. Talk to Dan. Maybe he can help you find Kelly."

"I don't need help finding him. I got a call from a colleague at the Met on the way over here. Apparently, someone with a high power hunting rifle blew half his head off a couple of hours ago. The last number he called was you."

Bill could feel his chest tightening. The room started to turn black around him and he had to fight to stay on his feet.

"Maybe he wanted to talk about Dan. Who knows. I didn't speak to him."

Mickey was watching his dad. He could see something was different about him. "Listen Holmes. Its time to leave. You can see my dad is upset about Sean."

Holmes looked at the old man. He seemed to have aged a hundred years in the last few minutes. "Ok, I'll be back tomorrow. I have lots of questions I need answered." He turned around and left just before Bill collapsed back into his chair breathing hard.

"Dad?"

"It's ok Mickey. I want you to arrange a car for me in the morning. I need to look Dan in the eyes when I ask him what the fuck he has been up to."

Mickey made a couple of calls. One to Slippery asking him to set up a visit and the other to Bill's driver.

"All done dad. Now, let's get you home. Maddy can lock up tonight." He lifted Bill and walked him slowly to the rear exit and his car.

Mickey had helped him to bed but sleep was impossible. The only rest he had was broken when he woke up in a cold sweat having a panic attack.

For the first time in his life he felt like things were out of control.

He needed to get a grip on his family as soon as possible. He showered and dressed. When Mickey arrived with his driver he told them he wanted to stop at Audrey's on the way to the prison.

"I need to make certain she is ok Mickey and then we can get over to Belmarsh."

Minutes later, the two of them left the car waiting outside and rang the doorbell. As it swung open, Ami stood inside with large circles under her eyes.

"Hello Bill. Come in. Everyone's in the kitchen. She turned and led them to the back of the house where Audrey was talking to Slippery.

"Audrey, Bill and Mickey are here. I need to go home to collect Olivia from her dad."

"Ok love. Thank you for coming round."

Bill stepped forward. "Let me arrange a car for you."

"No Bill, that's ok. I need to walk and think things through." She noticed his skin was ashen. "Audrey, can

I just pop up and see Theresa before I go."

"Yes, of course. I think she could do with seeing you."

Before she was halfway up the stairs Ami could hear the sobs coming from Sean's sisters room. She knocked on the door and walked in. Wrapped in a pile of sheets and shaking violently with every sucked breath, Theresa looked like a ghoul. Last nights mascara had run down her cheeks. Huge shadows were cast by Theresa's sunken eyes and her nose was running more than the sniffing could contain.

Ami sat on the bed and put her arms around her.

"It will get easier, I promise you. Sean loved you so much, you know that, don't you?"

Theresa sat up on the bed still sobbing, looking completely broken. "He was the only one I could trust, Ami. When he came home after splitting with Jean he always made me feel safe when he was near me. Like no one could ever hurt me. You're stronger than me, you probably wouldn't understand.

"I do, honey, I completely understand. But it will get better. Sean would be telling you the same if he was here."

Theresa hugged Ami back and it felt like a drowning person clinging to flotsam, desperately trying to keep from drowning.

Bill walked across the prison car park. He looked up at the entrance and rubbed the ball of his fist across his chest, the closer they got on the drive over, the more his heartburn was playing him up. In the last fifty years, very few things had scared him. Not the police, rival gangs or the IRA. But right now he would have paid good money not to have this conversation.

"You ok dad?"

"I'm ok Mickey. Just would prefer to be anywhere else than here. Wait in the car. I don't want you in the middle of this."

"I'll be right here when you get out dad."

Bill started to shamble slowly towards the gate but stopped after a few seconds. He turned around. "Mickey?"

"Yes dad."

"You've grown into a good man. I'm proud of you. When we were at Audrey's, I told Slippery to put you officially in charge of the business. Slippery has complete Power of Attorney and it will be legally filed by now."

"Dad…"

"I don't want Dan near the business. Ever. And if he admits that conversation with Kelly, I don't want him near me ever again. You understand Mickey?"

His son nodded and tried a smile as if to say thanks for trusting him, but in the state Bill looked it sucked all of the pride out of him and only left concern in it's place.

After a search and an I.D. check, Bill entered the visiting room. It was empty apart from the same guard as last time and Dan already sitting calmly at the table.

"Dan, I have some very sad news for you son."

Dan's excitement grew instantly. "What dad?"

"Sean was killed last night."

It was too much to control. Dan burst out laughing. "And that's sad? I don't think so. He deserved it."

"Dan that's your cousin. Our blood!"

"Not mine!"

"Dan, the police came to the club. They told me you had met with Kelly. Why?"

"I need him to help get me out. You and Slippery aren't doing shit!"

"Kelly doesn't do favours. Why should he help you?"

"Because I gave him a traitor. I gave him Sean!" Dan stood up laughing. "So I don't need you now."

The prison guard looked over at Dan, who remembered the beating he had the last time he shot his mouth off. He resumed his seat.

"My God... ...Dan! You? It was you?"

His son leant over the table and whispered. "Of course it was! Why are you so blind to it? We've hated each other for years! He's been nothing but a pain in my arse since he came back; always getting in to my business. My business dad! Who the fuck was he? A waste of space! He disrespected the family, our code, he buddies up with whoever, whenever. He's had no loyalty. A dog that has no loyalty needs to be put down, not pampered like the rest of ya have been doing. So I fucking sorted it, didn't I?! I. Put. Him. Down and now Kelly owes me."

"You fucking fool. Kelly's dead!" Bill grasped at his chest and his head fell in his hands.

Dan turned nearly as white as his father. "You ok dad?" Dan reached over the table but Bill threw his arm off and glared at his son.

"I'll never be OK, you little shit! You've killed my son! He was my son, just like you are. Sean was your brother!"

Dan laughed. "The famous O'Shea lies! They never end?" Then he saw the look in the old mans eyes and everything became clear. "That's why you treated him like you did? He could never do any wrong! I get it now. Golden boy! Not how ya treated me though, was it dad?"

"I treated you all the same. It's your fucked up head that sees everything through broken glass." His heart racing, he reached for Dan but his hand dropped through empty air as his chest screamed in agony. It felt like a knife had run through his left arm and a second later he crashed to the floor.

Dan dropped to the ground as the guard hit the panic alarm next to him. He ran over shouting "medical emergency" at the top of his voice and the room instantly filled with bodies all racing towards Bill.

FIFTEEN

As the ambulance raced through the streets, the blues and twos wailed and flashed separating the traffic in front of them. In the cab, the driver triggered the radio. "Bill O'Shea, suspected heart attack. Request team to meet us on arrival. E.T.A three minutes."

Exactly 2 minutes and forty eight seconds later, the ambulance pulled up and it was surrounded by staff who quickly wheeled Bill's lifeless body towards a cubical.

By two in the afternoon, the same people who were there the day before worried about Sean were sitting in virtually the same seats waiting for news about Bill.

A young doctor rounded the corner and came directly towards them. It was the same doctor who had looked after Sean.

"Hi," he said. "There might be a long wait. I wanted to keep you informed about Mr. O'Shea's condition. He is stable, but he has had a severe heart attack and we are going to send him up to intensive care."

Audrey decided to speak for the group. "Is he going to be OK?"

Mickey stood beside her. "He is, isn't he?"

The doctor put on his best bedside manner. "Look, I can't say one way or the other as it's very early days, but we have an excellent team looking after him. Go and have something to eat, freshen up and pop back later. Hopefully we will know more then."

"Audrey dismissed the idea. "No, we'll stay if you don't mind."

"That's fine, but you'll be more use to him if you all

go and get a good nights sleep.

Audrey ignored him and sat back down. "No, we're not going anywhere. When he needs us we'll be right here."

The doctor admitted defeat. It was obvious the Irish lady wasn't about to have her mind changed.

"There is one thing." He said. " Who's Ami?"

Everyone in the group turned and looked at her sitting in the corner.

Ami looked embarrassed. "I am."

"Mr O'Shea said he needs to speak to you but it would have to be very briefly. Just pop in for a few seconds."

Audrey and Mickey looked at each other as she was led away into the distance.

She was shown to a cubical at the far end of the corridor. "He's in here. Two minutes maximum."

Ami nodded and slid through the curtains.

She had tried to prepare herself but the body filled with tubes and electrodes looked like a different person to the one who offered her the use of his driver yesterday.

"Bill, you poor thing." She kissed him on the cheek and held his hand."

He drifted back into consciousness as he felt her touch him.

"He smiled weakly. "Ami, you should know something."

"Whatever it is it can wait until you are better.

"He became serious. "No, this cannot wait. I already waited too long."

"She sat beside him. Ok Bill. Tell me. What is it?"

"I was Sean's dad. I wish I'd told him, but it's too late now. I want you to tell his sons. I wish I could have told him too but it's too late for that. Make certain his boys know who their grandad is."

"Sean said his dad was killed by Ray."

"Ray was wrong. He thought it was someone else and he murdered him before Audrey and I could tell Ray the truth. Afterwards we just decided to let him think that. He never knew it was me."

Suddenly he gripped her hand as if he was about to fall and then all the strength left him. Alarms sounded from the machine by his side and within seconds Ami was bundled into the corridor outside.

Twenty minutes later, the same Doctor who pronounced Sean dead a day earlier, did the same for his father.

"Motherfuckers!"

Two inmates looked up towards the landing as a massive crash echoed from one of the cells. "Who's that?"

"Bill O'Shea's wanker of a son Dan. I think he just heard about his dad. News is he died on the operating table after that little shit caused him to have a heart attack."

"Bill O'Shea's dead? Fucking shame that. I remember the first time I was in. I had done some door work up west for him. Without asking, he kept an eye on my family and made certain they didn't go short. Last of the old school. I'll always owe him for that. So that little shit killed him?"

"A screw told me he was laughing at the old man as he was grabbing his chest on the floor."

"What a little fuck. We need a chat with him when all this shit dies down."

The other man nodded as three wardens ran into

Dan's cell.

"O'Shea! Calm down." The first one shouted as he pulled his baton. "I know you are upset but that won't stop us busting your face if you keep smashing your cell."

"Where's my fucking brief? I told you I need to see my brief!"

"Mr Shawcross arrived a few minutes ago. He's waiting to meet with you."

Dan took a breath and slowly walked to the door. Two of the officers walked him to a small meeting room near the main entrance.

Inside, Patrick Shawcross sat with a dark look on his face. It was part annoyance but mostly anger. "What do you want Dan?"

"I want to get out of here, that's what. When are you going to get me out Slippery?"

"I'm not."

Dan looked like the brief had pulled his own baton and smashed him in the face. "What the fuck do you mean Slippery? You're supposed to be getting me out!"

Patrick stood up. "Let me be clear Danny boy. My oldest friend is lying dead from a heart attack you bought on. You are showing no remorse whatsoever. People have told me that you arranged for Sean's death. All of this puts me in a particular mood to just say…" He left a pause of several seconds "…Fuck, you, Dan!"

Dan's face fell. The only person who could help him was now walking out of the door. "Slippery, come on…"

"That is Mr Shawcross to you." He paused in the doorway. "Perhaps you should talk to your friend Mr Kelly."

"Slipper... ...Mr Shawcross." Dan corrected himself. "Kelly's dead."

Patrick turned and as he breezed past the guard he said. "Exactly Dan and I think you will have a chance to catch up with him soon enough. Take this piece of shit back to the sewer please guard."

"No problem Mr Shawcross," said the officer smiling, "my pleasure."

The next day, Patrick Shawcross knocked on Audrey's door. He was not often surprised but the sight of a large distinguished Catholic Priest, dressed in black, opening the door to him, stopped him in his tracks. Eventually he recovered enough to say, "Good morning Father. My name is Shawcross. I am the family solicitor and Mrs O'Shea has asked me to take care of the funerals.

"Ah yes. She told me. Come on in. Her request is impossible I'm afraid."

"Yes, she said there was an issue. Issues are my speciality. Tell me how I can help."

The priest led the way to the living room where Audrey, Mickey, Theresa, Ami and Bill's wife were sitting.

"Look I'm afraid there are no places left in the part of the graveyard you want Sean and Bill buried. It is underneath an old tree where only members of the clergy are allowed to be laid to rest."

Ami poured Slippery a tea. "You see we would all like the two of them to be buried alongside each other Patrick," she said as she handed the cup over.

"Thank you Ami, you are a treasure. Audrey, is it ok if I help myself to one of your biscuits."

"Yes, of course Patrick, you know you don't need

to ask."

"Audrey," said Patrick as he leaned back in his chair and dipped his biscuit into the cup. "It would be very wrong of me if I just helped myself to one of your biscuits without asking. In fact I find it very dishonourable, if not criminal, when people help themselves to things they are not entitled. Why it would be like the Father here dipping his hand in the collection tray to fund a secret gambling habit, and no-one would condone behaviour like that would they?"

All the eyes in the room turned towards the clergyman. His cheeks had flushed and a sweat had instantly broken out on his forehead.

Slippery leant forward, picked up the plate and said "Biscuit Father?"

"Er no," he said jumping to his feet. "I just remembered, we could find a way to make an exception for good standing members of the community like Mr O'Shea. I have to go and make some calls but I am certain it will not be an issue. Good morning and good bless everyone." He disappeared in a cloud of dog collars and sweat.

Everyone looked at Slippery and tried to imagine they hadn't just seen him blackmail a man of the cloth in broad daylight. He popped the biscuit in his mouth. "Lubbly," he mumbled as he sipped his tea.

An hour later, Patrick had taken all the details he needed to make the plans. "I think I have everything so I can leave you all in piece. Ami, would you walk me to the door."

Audrey kissed him on the cheek. "Thanks Patrick, you are one of a kind."

He held Ami's hand as he walked to the front door but when he got there he pulled her gently through it and to his car.

"Sean wanted you to have this." He opened the boot and handed over an A4 box about three inches deep. She looked inside and smiled.

"Thank you Patrick. You are a star as always."

"Just closing some open doors, that's all."

He climbed in his car and waved out of the window as he disappeared from view.

Everyone was wearing black. The ladies all had black dresses, black shoes and black glasses. The men all had black suits and matching ties. A light drizzle meant the air around the grave was full of black umbrellas and just so it wasn't left out, the sky turned dark as they lowered the two black coffins into the ground.

The O'Shea family, supported by their friend Patrick Shawcross, and presided over by a very nervous priest, all threw dirt into the graves.

Theresa held Ami's hand one side as Olivia held her mother's the other.

In the distance, Ami noticed Serj standing with his arm around Tasha. Ami guessed she had decided not to create a drama but to, instead, watch from a distance. She smiled at her and Tasha nodded back.

Suddenly the quiet was shattered by a turbo diesel engine dragging a lot of bullet proof glass and steel. The prison van parked at the far end of the funeral procession and a man was bundled out in handcuffs flanked by two guards.

Dan's smiling face came into view.

Audrey and Mickey broke away from the crowd and stormed over.

She stood in front of the prisoner who was being

held back at a safe distance by one of the officers. Audrey spat in his face to bridge the gap. "How dare you show up here! You are an embarrassment to the O'Shea name. You're the reason we are burying them!"

Dan wiped away the bile and grinned. "Tough shit. I came to dance on Sean's grave."

Audrey lunged forward to slap him but Mickey caught her.

"Mickey, get him out of my sight before I put him in the ground next to them," and she walked back to the other mourners.

Mickey stepped forward into his brother's face. "You just couldn't leave it, could you? You deserve everything you get." Mickey nodded to the prison guards. "This man isn't welcome here. This is for O'Shea family members only.

They started to pull Dan's arms. "Get off me! I need to speak to my family, I have rights! Mickey! Mickey! Come on, you're my brother Mickey. Sort me out. Make Slippery help me!"

The younger man turned to face his brother. "It's Michael to you. Enjoy life inside. What little you have left."

Ami's hand appeared on Mickey's shoulder as Dan was dragged back towards the van. Just as he was pulled into the road, a blacked out limo rolled past with the driver window wound down. Inside Dan recognised the youngest Dolan brother.

"What the fuck?" He turned and saw Ami nod towards the driver as he waved back. Ami turned back to Dan and smiled.

The car pulled to a stop and Serj climbed into the front passenger seat. Ami walked over with Olivia in tow and climbed in the back. Tasha stood at the opposite door as Serj leaned back and opened it for her. "Wait," she said. "I need to say something." Deliberately, she walked towards the men dragging Dan back to the prison transport.

"I know what you were trying to do to me. I pieced it together after I got straight. I'm glad the last thing you will see is my face before you go down."

Dan struggled forward but one of the guards rabbit-punched him in the kidney and he dropped to his knees, gasping. "This isn't over you little slut!"

Tasha stepped close and whispered in his ear, "Oh I think it is. I'll be sure to let Sean know you said "hi" when I see him." She slapped him hard and quickly stepped back.

"What? You bitch! Let me go! Let me fucking kill her!"

The guards lost their patience and dragged him screaming to the back doors and let him fall hard on his face as he was thrown in. Just as the doors closed he watched Tasha slide into the limo as it pulled out away from the curb. "Nooooo!" he screamed.

Serj looked across at Dolan. You cut it close my friend. When you sped past on the motorbike, guns blazing, one of the bullets shattered two ribs through the kevlar vest. My man is strapped up and high on pain killers."

"Could be worse. It could have been someone else who stepped out of the shadows rather than me. Kelly had put enough on the Irishman's head to have people queuing around the block. Luckily I got there first."

"Mickey is expecting a call about a joint business venture between the two families. Don't fuck it up. Now your organisation is clean and your informant is under Sean's headstone, you two should make a fortune if you don't get greedy. Now, a quick stop and then onto the airport with this lot in the back."

At Heathrow the limo pulled up at the drop off point. Serj opened the back door and two small boys stepped out followed by Ami, Olivia and Tasha.
He loaded a couple of suitcases onto a trolley and then pushed it to the entrance for them.
"I'll see you in two weeks, all things being equal. Have a good flight."
Ami kissed him on the cheek. "Thank you Serj. Keep safe."
Tasha jumped forward and kissed him hard on the lips.
Serj fell back when she released him. "It won't be very safe for me if you do that in front of your dad."
Tasha waved and held Olivia's hand as Ami and the boys pushed the trolley to the check in.
A tall man was chatting to the young female clerk.
Ami walked over and put an A4 box on the counter next to him. "You won't get far without the tickets and passports honey," she said and kissed him on the lips. "Uncle Patrick says have a great trip. Your mum played the part brilliantly and now she will tell Theresa."
Sean opened the box and flicked through six passports each with one of their photos in. Under them all was the name Richards.
"Well Mrs Richards, shall we?" He handed the passports over as his boys grabbed his legs from behind. He looked around him.
"Family," he said and started negotiating an upgrade to first class.

The End

ABOUT THE AUTHOR

Luing Andrews, accomplished actor, writer and director, works on both sides of the Atlantic.

He grew up in London and learnt the art of boxing from a very early age. From there he trained in several forms of martial arts including kick boxing. Over the years he made a name for himself, winning tournaments in each successive discipline.

His success gained considerable interest from directors and started his career as a stunt performer. From there, he managed to move into acting and has featured in productions in America and the UK.

This book is very much how his London was and still is.

8ish was originally written as a 90 minute feature film script by Luing, proceeds from this novel will help towards the funding and realising his dreams of creating a fantastic British film.

Printed in Great Britain
by Amazon